Denver Post:
"A WILD RIDE, FROM THE IVIED HALLS
OF SOUTHERN ACADEMIA TO THE
CRASHING BIG SUR SURF."

Toronto Star:
"This novel is hard to set aside. Patterson's complex tale chills, enthralls, and entertains the reader in A DAZZLING AND UNFORGETTABLE READING EXPERIENCE."

Grand Rapids Press:
"Robert B. Parker's Spenser, Patricia Cornwell's Kay Scarpetto, and Evan Hunter's 87th Precinct Detectives. . . . IT'S TIME TO GET OUT THE PARTY HATS, WELCOME JAMES PATTERSON TO THE CLUB."

Baton Rouge Magazine:
"A TENSE, COMPLEX PLOT OF ABDUCTION AND MURDER THAT IS HARD TO PUT DOWN. THE READER IS HOOKED FROM PAGE ONE. . . . This is a crime story so scary it will hold the reader's attention and leave a lingering horror at the back of the mind for days."

West Coast Review of Books:
"AN ENJOYABLE READ, WRITTEN IN CONCISE, PITHY LANGUAGE THAT MOVES AS GRACEFULLY AS IF WE WERE WATCHING IT ON WIDE SCREEN AT THE LOCAL THEATER."

more . . .

272·4535

YOU ARE ABOUT TO BEGIN ONE OF THE CLASSIC AMERICAN NOVELS OF SUSPENSE.

THE *NEW YORK TIMES* CALLS *THE THOMAS BERRYMAN NUMBER* "SURE-FIRE!" IT IS.

John D. MacDonald, creator of Travis McGee:
"TOUGH, WRY, AND ELOQUENT."

Library Journal:
"BRILLIANTLY WRITTEN!"

Richard Condon, author of *The Manchurian Candidate*:
"WHAT A LARGE CHARGE IT IS TO COME UPON SUCH A GOOD WRITER. . . . The novel tells a lot about many things but most of all about America in the last quarter of the 20th century."

Robin Moore, author of *The French Connection*:
"HURRAY! ONCE YOU READ PAGE ONE YOU WILL NOT STOP UNTIL YOU HAVE FINISHED."

New York Times:
"JAMES PATTERSON DOES EVERYTHING BUT STICK OUR FINGER INTO A LIGHT SOCKET TO GIVE US A BUZZ."

more . . .

Books by JAMES PATTERSON

THE THOMAS
BERRYMAN
NUMBER

JAMES PATTERSON

WARNER BOOKS

A Time Warner Company

The author is grateful to Warner Bros. Music for permission to quote excerpted lyrics from "Ballad of a Thin Man" by Bob Dylan. Copyright © 1965 M. Witmark & Sons. All rights reserved.

WARNER BOOKS EDITION

Published by arrangement with Little, Brown and Company.

Cover design by Steve Snider
Cover illustration by Joe Ovis
Hand lettering by Anthony C. Russo

Warner Books, Inc.
1271 Avenue of the America
New York, NY 10020

Visit our Web site at
www.warnerbooks.com

W A Time Warner Company

Printed in the United States of America

First Warner Books Printing: April, 1996

15

THE THOMAS BERRYMAN NUMBER

PROLOGUE

Down on the Farm (1962)

Claude, Texas, 1962

The year he and Ben Toy left Claude, Texas—1962—
Thomas Berryman had been in the habit of wearing black
cowboy boots with distinctive red stars on the ankles.
He'd also been stuffing four twenty-dollar bills in each
boot sole. By mid-July the money had begun to shred and
smell like feet.

One otherwise unpromising afternoon there'd been a
shiny Coupe de Ville out on Ranch Road #5. It was metallic blue. Throwing sun spirals and stars off the bumpers.

He and Ben Toy had watched its approach for six or
eight miles of scruffy Panhandle desert. They were doing
nothing. "Bored sick and dying fast on a fencerail,"
Berryman had said earlier. Toy had only half-smiled.

"You heard about that greaseball Raymond Cone? I
suppose you did," the conversation was going now.

"I always said that was going to happen." Berryman
puffed thoughtfully on a non-filter cigarette. "The way

he's always talking about dry-humping Nadine in his old man's Chevrolet, it had to."

"You think he'll marry her?"

"I *know* he'll marry her. It's been happening for about a hundred years straight around here. Then the old man gets him with Pepsi in Amarillo. Then she has the kid. Then he splits on both of them for Reno, Nevada, or California. I hate that, I really do."

Toy took out a small, wrinkled roll of money and started counting five- and ten- and one-dollar bills. "He says he'll put a 30-30 in his mouth. Before he marries Nadine."

"Yeah, well ... He'll be haulassing soda cases pretty soon. That'll dilute his 'Frankie and Johnny' philosophies."

Thomas Berryman shaded his sunglasses so he could see the approaching car better. A finely made coil of brown dust followed it like a streamer. Buzzards crossed its path, heading east toward Wichita Falls.

When the Coupe was less than twenty-five yards away, Berryman flipped out his thumb. "Are you coming or not?" he said to Toy.

The big car, meanwhile, had clicked out of cruise-control and was easing to a stop.

The driver turned out to be the Bishop of Albuquerque. Padre Luis Gonsolo. Both young men left Claude, Texas, with him. They kept right on going until they were in New York City.

Thomas Berryman and Ben Toy rode into New York in high style too . . . in the 1962 metallic blue Coupe de Ville . . . without the Bishop.

PREFACE

Jones' Thomas Berryman (1974)

> My parents, Walter and Edna Linda Jones, didn't want me to be a doctor, or a lawyer, or even successful; they just wanted me to be refined . . . I disappointed them badly, however; I went out and became a newspaperman.

> SIGN OVER THE DESK OF OCHS JONES

> Steve McQueen is a killer
> you have to cheer on and root for.
> NEWSPAPER MOVIE REVIEW

Zebulon, Kentucky, 1974

In November of this year I came back to my hometown (Zebulon) in Poland County, Kentucky; I came home to write about the deaths of men named Bertram Poole, Lieutenant Martin Weesner, and especially my friend Jimmie Lee Horn of Nashville, Tennessee . . . but most of all I came home to write about something an editor at the *Nashville Citizen-Reporter* had named the Thomas Berryman Number.

This book is mostly for my nine-year-old daughter Cat, I think.

It's a Sam Peckinpah kind of story: all in all there are six murders in it. It's about a young Texas man who decided to become a professional killer at the age of eighteen. So far as I can make out, he decided by virtue of executing several beautiful pronghorn antelopes and one Mexican priest, a bishop actually.

Random observation: A story in a Houston paper reports that *"Not less than five men in the United States are making over two hundred thousand dollars a year as independent (non-mob) assassins."* What the hell is the point of view over in Houston I wondered when I cut out the clipping and folded it for my wallet.

Random observation: Very few people have understood the character of men who do evil . . . Most people who've written about them just make everything too black for me. Either that, or they're trying to make some sugar and spice "Bonnie & Clyde" movie . . . Anyway, movie stars withstanding, I don't believe your bad man can be obtuse, and

I don't believe he'd necessarily be morose ... In fact, Thomas Berryman was neither of these.

Random observation: The other day, I showed Cat something Berryman's girlfriend had given me: it was a Crossman air pistol. To demonstrate how it could put someone to sleep, I callously (stupidly) wounded Mrs. Mullhouse's calico. It was too much for the old kitty, however, and she died.

Random observation: Even Doc Fiddler's Paradise Lounge, one of the top redneck gin mills in the state of Tennessee, has a fresh print of Jimmie Horn over the liquor these days. Horn's strictly moral drama now, and people are partial to moral drama, no matter what.

One last observation: In 1962, Thomas John Berryman graduated from Plains High School with one of the highest grade point averages ever recorded in Potter County, Texas. Some teachers said he had a photographic memory, and he had a measured I.Q. of one hundred sixty-six.

A little more digging revealed that he was known as the "Pleasure King," and nicknamed "Pleasure."

The women who'd been his girlfriends would only say that he made them feel inferior. Even the ones who'd liked him best never felt totally comfortable with him.

Most people around Clyde, Texas, thought he was a successful lawyer in the East now. At first I'd thought someone in the Berryman family started the rumor; later on, I'd learned it had been Berryman himself.

Berryman's father was a retired circuit judge. Three weeks after he learned what his son had done in Tennessee, he died of a cerebrovascular accident.

Thomas Berryman is 6′1″, one hundred ninety-five pounds. He has black hair, hazel eyes. And extremely good concentration for a young man. He's also charming. In fact, he just about says it all for American charm.

Background: Four months ago, the thirty-seven-year-old mayor of our city, Jimmie Horn, was shot down under the saddest and most bizarre circumstances I can imagine.

Because of that, the *Nashville Citizen-Reporter*s of last July 4th, 5th, and 6th are the three largest-selling editions the paper has ever had.

Maybe it's because people are naturally curious when public figures are shot. They know casual facts out of their lives, and they regard these men almost as acquaintances. They want to know how, and where, and what time, and why it happened.

I believe it's usually the same: *madman Bert Poole shoots Mayor Jimmie Horn, late in the day for no good reason.*

That's what I wrote, but only in pencil on foolscap. In the *Citizen*, I wrote a long filler about the state trooper who'd subsequently shot Poole.

It was real shit, and also crass ... It was also incorrect.

Three days after the shooting, a story in the *Washington Post* reported that the man who'd shot Bert Poole hadn't been a Tennessee state trooper as my story, and our other feature stories, had reported several times.

The man was an expensive professional killer from Philadelphia. His name was Joe Cubbah. Cubbah had been spotted in photographs of the Horn shooting; then he'd been picked up in Philadelphia.

The real Tennessee trooper, Martin Weesner, was finally found in the trunk of his own squad car. The car had been in a trooper barracks parking lot since July 3rd. Cubbah was called "an imaginative gunman" by the *Memphis Times-Scimitar*.

Needless to say, this matter of a professional killer shooting down an assassin confused the hell out of everybody. It also depressed a good number of people, myself included. And it scared a lot of families into locking their doors at night.

Coincidentally, during the wake of the *Washington Post* story, the *Citizen-Reporter* received an hour-long phone call from a resident psychiatrist working at a Long Island, N.Y., hospital. The doctor explained to one of our editors how a patient of his had been talking about the Jimmie Horn shooting nearly a week before it happened. He gave out the patient's name as Ben Toy, and he said it was fine if we wanted to send someone around to talk with him.

We wanted to send me, and that's how I fit into the story.

As a consequence of that decision, I'm now sequestered away in a Victorian farmhouse outside of Zebulon, in Poland County. It's November now as I mentioned.

I'd thought that I would enjoy hunting down the murderer of a friend—delicious revenge, they say—but I was wrong.

From 4 A.M. until around eleven each day I try to collate, then make sense out of the over two thousand pages of notes, scraps, and interview transcripts that recreate the days leading up to the Horn shooting this past July.

I've already made an indecent amount of money from advances, magazine sales, and newspaper serials on Thomas Berryman stories. This is the book.

PART I

The First Trip North

West Hampton, July 9

In nineteen sixty-nine I won a George Polk prize for some life-style articles about black Mayor Jimmie Lee Horn of Nashville. The series was called "A Walker's Guide to Shantytown," but it ran in the *Citizen-Reporter* as "Black Lives."

It wasn't a bad writing job, but it was more a case of being in the right place at the right time: I'd written life-affirming stories about a black man in Tennessee, just a year after Martin Luther King had died there.

It felt right to people who judged things somewhere. They said the series was "vital."

So I was lucky in '69.

I figured things were beginning to even out the day I drove into the William Pound Institute in West Hampton, Long Island. On account of my assignment there I wouldn't be writing any of the article about Horn's murder. The good Horn assignments had already gone elsewhere. Higher up.

I parked my rent-a-car in a crowded yard marked ALL HOSPITAL VISITORS ALL. Then, armed with tape recorder, suitcoat over my arm too, I made my way along a broken flagstone path tunneling through bent old oak trees.

I didn't really notice a lot about the hospital at first. I was busy feeling sorry for myself.

Random Observation: The man looking most obviously lost and disturbed at the William Pound Institute— baggy white suit, torn panama hat, Monkey Ward dress shirt—must have been me.

Here was Ochs Jones, thirty-one-year-old cornpone savant, never before having been north of Washington D.C.

But the Brooks Brothers doctors, the nurses, the fire-haired patients walking around the hospital paid no attention.

Which isn't easy—even at 9:30 on a drizzly, unfriendly morning.

Generally I'm noticed most places.

My blond hair is close-cropped, just a little seedy on the sides, already falling out on top—so that my head resembles a Franciscan monk's. I'm slightly cross-eyed without my glasses (and because of the rain I had them off). Moreover, I'm 6'7", and I stand out quite nicely without the aid of quirky clothes.

No one noticed, though. One doctory-looking woman

said, "Hello, Michael." "Ochs," I told her. That was about it for introductions.

Less than 1% believing Ben Toy might have a story for me, I dutifully followed all the blue-arrowed signs marked BOWDITCH.

The grounds of the Pound Institute were clean and fresh-smelling and green as a state park. The hospital reminded me of an eastern university campus, someplace with a name like Ithaca, or Swarthmore, or Hobart.

It was nearly ten as I walked past huge red-brick houses along an equally red cobblestone road.

Occasionally a Cadillac or Mercedes crept by at the posted ten m.p.h. speed limit.

The federalist-style houses I passed were the different wards of the hospital.

One was for the elderly bedridden. Another was for the elderly who could still putter around—predominantly lobotomies.

One four-story building housed nothing but children aged over ten years. A little girl sat rocking in the window of one of the downstairs rooms. She reminded me of Anthony Perkins at the end of *Psycho*.

I jotted down a few observations and felt silly making them. I kept one wandering eye peeled for Ben Toy's ward: Bowditch: male maximum security.

A curious thing happened to me in front of the ward for young girls.

A round-shouldered girl was sitting on the wet front lawn close to the road where I was walking. She was playing a blond-wood guitar and singing.

There's something goin' on, she just about talked the pop song.
But you don't know what it is,
Do you, Mr. Jones?

I was Ochs Jones, thirty-one, father of two daughters . . . The only violent act I could recall in my life, was *hearing*—as a boy—that my great-uncle Ochs Jones had been hanged in Moon, Kentucky, as a horsethief . . . and *no*, I didn't know what was going on.

As a matter of fact, I knew considerably less than I thought I did.

• • •

The last of the Federal-style houses was more rambling, less formal and kept-up than any of the others. It bordered on scrub pine woods with very green waist-high underbrush running through it. A high stockade fence had been built up as the ward's backyard.

BOWDITCH a fancy gold plaque by the front door said.

The man who'd contacted the *Citizen-Reporter*, Dr. Alan Shulman, met me on the front porch. Right off, Shulman informed me that this was an unusual and delicate situation for him. The hospital, he said, had only divulged information about patients a few times before—

and that invariably had to do with court cases. "But an assassination," he said, "is somewhat extraordinary. We *want* to help."

Shulman was very New Yorkerish, with curly, scraggly black hair. He wore the kind of black-frame eyeglasses with little silver arrows in the corners. He was probably in his mid-thirties, with some kind of Brooklyn or Queens accent that was odd to my ear.

Some men slouching inside behind steel-screened windows seemed to be finding us quite a curious combination to observe.

A steady flow of collected rainwater rattled the drainpipe on the porch.

It made it a little harder for Shulman and myself to hear one another's side of the argument that was developing.

"I left my home around five, five-fifteen this morning," I said in a quick, agitated bluegrass drawl.

"I took an awful Southern Airways flight up to Kennedy Airport . . . awful flight . . . stopped at places like Dohren, Alabama . . . Then I drove an Econo-Car out to God-knows-where-but-I-don't, Long Island. And now, you're not going to let me in to see Toy . . . Is that right Doctor Shulman? That's right, isn't it?"

Shulman just nodded the curly black head.

Then he said something like this to me: "Ben Toy had a very bad, piss-poor night last night. He's been up and down since he got in here . . . I think he *wants* to get better now . . . I don't think he wants to kill himself right now ... So maybe you can talk with him tomorrow. Maybe even tonight. Not now, though."

"Aw shit," I shook my head. I loosened up my tie and a laugh snorted out through my nose. The laugh is a big flaw in my business style. I can't really take myself too seriously, and it shows.

When Shulman laughed too I started to like him. He had a good way of laughing that was hard to stay pissed off at. I imagined he used it on all his patients.

"Well, at least invite me in for some damn coffee," I grinned.

The doctor took me into a back door through Bowditch's nurse's station.

I caught a glimpse of nurses, some patients, and a lot of Plexiglas surrounding the station. We entered another room, a wood-paneled conference room, and Shulman personally mixed me some Sanka.

After some general small talk, he told me why he'd started to feel that Ben Toy was somehow involved in the murders of Jimmie Horn, Bert Poole, and Lieutenant Mart Weesner.

I told him why most of the people at the *Citizen* doubted it.

Our reasons had to do with motion pictures of the Horn shooting. The films clearly showed young Poole shooting Horn in the chest and face.

Alan Shulman's reasons had to do with gut feelings. (And also with the nagging fact that the police would probably never remove Ben Toy from an institution to face trial.)

Like the man or not, I was not overly impressed with his theories.

"Don't you worry," he assured me, "this story will be worth your time and air fare ... if you handle it right."

As part of the idea of getting my money's worth out of the trip, I drove about six miles south after leaving the hospital.

I slipped into a pair of cut-offs in my rent-a-car, then went for my first swim in an ocean.

If I'd known how little time I'd be having for the next five months, I would have squeezed even more out of the free afternoon.

• • •

The rainy day turned into beautiful, pink-and-blue-skied night.

I was wearing bluejeans and white shirttails, walking down the hospital's cobblestone road again. It was 8:30 that same evening and I'd been asked to come back to Bowditch.

A bear-bearded, rabbinical-looking attendant was assigned to record and supervise my visit with Ben Toy. A ring of keys and metal badges jangled from the rope belt around his Levi's. A plastic name pin said that he was MR. RONALD ASHER, SENIOR MENTAL HEALTH WORKER.

The two of us, both carrying pads and pencils, walked down a long, gray-carpeted hall with airy, white-curtained bedrooms on either side.

Something about being locked in the hall made me a little tense. I was combing my hair with my fingers as I walked along.

"Our quiet room's about the size of a den," Asher told me. "It's a seclusion room. Seclusion room's used for patients who act-out violently. Act-out against the staff, or other patients, or against themselves."

"Which did Ben Toy do?" I asked the attendant.

"Oh shit." Big white teeth showed in his beard. "He's been in there for all three at one time or another. He can be a total jerk-off, and then again he can be a pretty nice guy."

Asher stopped in front of the one closed door in the hallway. While he opened it with two different keys, I looked inside through a book-sized observation window.

The room *was* tiny.

It had gunboat metal screens and red bars on small, mud-spattered windows. A half-eaten bowl of cereal and milk was on the windowsill. Outside was the stockade wall and an exercise yard.

Ben Toy was seated on the room's only furniture, a narrow blue pinstriped mattress. He was wearing a black cowboy Stetson, but when he saw my face in the window he took it off.

"Come on the hell in," I heard a friendly, muffled voice. "The door's only triple-locked."

Just then Asher opened it.

Ben Toy was a tall, thin man, about thirty, with a fast, easy, hustler's smile. His blond hair was oily, unwashed. He was Jon Voight on the skids.

Toy was wearing white pajama bottoms with no top. His ribs were sticking out to be counted. His chest was covered with curly, auburn hair, however, and he was basically rugged-looking.

According to Asher, Toy had tried to starve himself when he'd first come in the hospital. Asher said he'd been burly back then.

When Toy spoke his voice was soft. He seemed to be trying to sound hip. N.Y.-L.A. dope world sounds.

"You look like a Christian monk, man," he drawled pleasantly.

"No shit," I laughed, and he laughed too. He seemed pretty normal. Either that, or the black-bearded aide was a snake charmer.

After a little bit of measuring each other up, Toy and I went right into Jimmie Horn.

Actually, I started on the subject, but Toy did most of the talking.

He knew what Horn looked like; where Horn had lived; precisely where his campaign headquarters had been. He knew the names of Jimmie Horn's two children; his parents' names; all sorts of impossible trivia nobody outside of Tennessee would have any interest in.

At that point, I found myself talking rapidly and listening very closely. The Sony was burning up tape.

"You think you know who shot Horn up?" Toy said to me.

"I think I do, yes. A man named Bert Poole shot him. A chronic bumbler who lived in Nashville all his life. A fuck-up."

"This *bumbler*," Toy asked. "How did you figure out he did it?"

His question was very serious; forensic, in a country pool hall way. He was slowly turning the black Stetson around on his fist.

"For one thing," I said, "I saw it on television. For another thing, I've talked to a shitload of people who were there."

Toy frowned at me. "Guess you talked to the wrong shitload of people," he said. He was acting very sure of himself.

It was just after that when Toy spoke of the contact, or bagman, involved with Jimmie Horn.

It was then also that I heard the name Thomas Berryman for the first time.

Provincetown, June 6

The time Toy spoke of was early June of that year; the place was Provincetown, Massachusetts.

Young Harley John Wynn parked in the shadows behind the Provincetown City Hall and started off toward

Commercial Street with visions of power and money dancing in his head. Wynn was handsome, fair and baby-faced like the early F. Scott Fitzgerald photographs. His car was a Lincoln Mark IV. In some ways he was like Thomas Berryman. Both men were thoroughly modern, coldly sober, distressingly sure of themselves.

For over three weeks, Harley Wynn had been making enquiries about Berryman. He'd finally been contacted the Tuesday before that weekend.

The meeting had been set up for Provincetown. Wynn was asked to be reading a *Boston Globe* on one of the benches in front of the City Hall at 9:45 p.m.

It was almost 9:30, and cool, even for Cape Cod in June.

The grass was freshly mown, and it had a good smell for Wynn: it reminded him of college quadrangles in the deep South. Cape Cod itself reminded him of poliomyelitis.

Careful of his shoeshine, he stayed in tree shadows just off the edge of the lawn. He sidestepped a snake, which turned out to be a tangle of electrician's tape.

He was startled by some green willow fingers, and realized he was still in a driving fog.

It wasn't night on Commercial Street, and as Wynn came into the amber lights he began to smell light cologne instead of sod.

He sat on one of the freshly painted benches—bone

white, like the City Hall—and he saw that he was among male and female homosexuals.

There were several tall blonds in scarlet and powder blue halter suits. Small, bushy-haired men in white bucks and thongs, and bright sailor-style pants. There were tank-shirts and flapping sandals and New York *Times* magazine models posing under street-lamps.

Wynn lighted a Marlboro, noticed uneasiness in his big hands, and took a long, deep breath.

He looked up and down the street for Ben Toy.

Up on the porch of the City Hall, his eyes stopped to watch flour-white gargoyles and witchy teenagers parading to and from the public toilets.

Harley Wynn's hand kept slipping inside his suitjacket and touching a thick, brown envelope.

Across the street, Ben Toy, thirty, and Thomas Berryman, twenty-nine, were sitting together drinking beer and Taylor Cream in a rear alcove of the A. J. Fogarty bar.

Rough-hewn men with expensive sunglasses, they brought to mind tennis bums.

They were talking about Texas with two Irish girls they'd discovered in Hyannis. One girl wore a tartan skirt and top; the other was wearing a pea-coat, rolled-up jeans, and striped baseball-player socks.

Toy and Berryman told old Texas stories back and forth, and listened to less-polished but promising Boston tales.

Oona, the taller, prettier girl, was telling how she sometimes walked Massachusetts Avenue in Boston, pretending she was a paraplegic. "Like all these business types from the Pru," she said, "they get too embarrassed to ogle. I can be by myself if I want to."

Thomas Berryman stared at her boozily with great red eyes. "That's a very funny bit," he smiled slightly. Then he was tilting his head back and forth with the pendulum of a Miller beer clock.

It was ten o'clock. Miller's was still the champagne of bottled beers. Bette Midler was singing boogie on the jukebox.

A handsome blond man was talking to Oona from a stool at the bar. "You know who you remind me of," he smiled brightly, "you remind me of Lauren Hutton."

"Excuse me," the tall girl smiled back innocently, "but you've obviously mistaken me for someone who gives a shit."

This time Berryman laughed out loud. All of them did.

Then Berryman spoke quietly to Ben Toy. "Don't you think he's been waiting long enough now?"

Toy licked beer foam off his upper lip. "No," he said. "Hell no."

"You're sure about that, Ben? Got it buttoned up for me? . . ."

"The man's just getting uncomfortable about now. Taking an occasional deep breath. Getting real p.o.'d at me. I want him good and squirmy when I go talk to him . . . Besides though, I don't need this paranoia shit."

Berryman grinned at him. "Just checking," he said. "So long as you deliver, you do it any way you want to."

At 10:30, forty-five minutes after the arranged time, Ben Toy got up and slowly walked up to A. J. Fogarty's front window.

He was later to remember watching Wynn through the Calligraphia window lettering. Wynn in an expensive blue suit with gray pinstripes. Wynn in brown Florsheim tie shoes and a matching brown belt. Southern macho, Toy thought.

For his part, Ben Toy was wearing a blue muslin shirt with a red butterfly design on the back. With pearl snaps. He was a big, blue-eyed man; Berryman's back-up; Berryman's old friend from Texas; a Texas rake.

Among boys in Amarillo, Ben Toy had once been known as "the funniest man in America."

He smiled now as Wynn started to read the *Boston Globe* again. The money was apparently in his left side jacket pocket. He kept rubbing his elbow up against it.

Harley John Wynn couldn't have helped noticing Toy as he left Fogarty's bar. Toy looked like a drunken lord: he had long blond hair, and an untroubled face.

He walked slowly behind a college boy in a mauve Boston College sweatshirt. He waded through various kinds of Volkswagens on the street; then he calmly sat down on Harley Wynn's bench.

• • •

In his own right, southern lawyer Harley Wynn was a cool, collected, and moderately successful young man. He knew himself to be clearheaded and analytical. He identified with men like Bernie Cornfeld and Robert Yablans—the brash, bootleg quarterback types in the business world. Now he was making a big play of his own.

Wynn's generally *together* appearance didn't fool Ben Toy, however. The southern man's hands had given him away. They were sweaty, and had taken newspaper print up off the *Boston Globe*. Telltale smudges were on his forehead and right on the tip of his nose.

"I was just thinking about all of this," Wynn gestured around the street and environs. "The fact that you're nearly an hour late. The faggots . . . You're trying very hard to put me at a disadvantage." The southerner smiled boyishly. He held out an athletic-looking hand. "I approve of that," he said.

Ben Toy ignored the outstretched hand. He grunted indifferently and looked down at his boottips.

Harley Wynn laughed at the way nervous men try to condescend.

Toy still said nothing.

"All right then," Wynn's southern twang stiffened. ". . . Horn's a fairly intelligent nigger . . . Very intelligent, matter of fact."

Toy looked up and established eye contact with the man.

"Horn has affronted sensibilities in the South, however. That's neither here nor there. My interest in the matter, your interest, is purely monetary." He looked for some nod of agreement from Ben Toy.

"I don't have anything to say to that," Toy finally

spoke. He lighted a cigarette, spread his long, blue-jeaned legs, sat back on the bench and watched traffic.

The young lawyer began to force smiles. He was capable of getting quick acceptance and he was overly used to it. He glanced to where Toy was looking, expecting someone else to join them.

"You'll be provided with detailed information on Horn," he said. "Daily routines and schedules if you like . . ." The lawyer spewed out information like a computer.

"All right, stop it now." Toy finally swung around and looked at Wynn again. His teeth were clenched tight.

He jabbed the man in the stomach with his fist. "I could kill you, man," he said. "Stop fucking around with me."

The lawyer was pale, perspiring at the hairline. He wasn't comprehending.

Toy cleared his throat before he spoke again. He spit up an impressive gob on the lawn. Headlights went across Harley Wynn's eyes, then over his own.

"Berryman wants a reason," he said. "He wants to know exactly why you're offering all this money."

Toy cautioned Harley Wynn with his finger before he let him answer. "Don't fuck with me."

"I haven't been fucking with you," Wynn said. "I understand the seriousness of this. The precautions . . . In fact, that's the explanation you want . . . There can be no suspicions after this thing is over with. No loose ends. This isn't a simple matter of killing Horn. My people are vulnerable to suspicion. They want no questions asked of them afterward."

Ben Toy smiled at the lawyer's answer. He slid over closer to Wynn. He put his arm around the pin-striped suit. This was where he earned all his pay.

"Then I think we've had enough Looney Tunes for tonight," he said in a soft, Texas drawl. "You owe us half of our money as of right now. You have the money inside your jacket."

Wynn tried to pull away, "I was told I'd get to talk with Berryman himself," he protested.

"You just give me the money you're supposed to have," Toy said. "The money or I leave. No more talk."

The southern man hesitated, but he finally took out the brown envelope. The contact was completed.

Ben Toy walked away with fifty thousand dollars stuffed around his dungarees. He was feeling very good about himself.

Over his head the City Hall clock sounded like it was floating in the sky. *Bongg. Bongg. Bongg.*

Inside the pub window Thomas Berryman was clicking off important photographs of Harley John Wynn.

The Thomas Berryman Number had begun.

New York City, June 12

Six days after the first exchange of money, a white pigeon walked down Central Park South in New York City, stopped to taste a soggy wad of Kleenex, then flew up to the granite ledge surrounding the windows of Thomas Berryman's apartment.

Berryman says there are always pathetic city pigeons perched on his ledge. And that they'll never look in at him or anyone else.

There are also long cigarillo ends all over the ledge.

And there's an old Texarkana trick of burning off bird feathers with cigars.

The window is up ten stories over Central Park South. The building is picturesque, a dark, towering graystone hotel.

A famous fascist banker once killed himself out of one of the nearby floor-to-ceiling windows. He tied a rope to a radiator, jumped, hanged himself.

Because his neck is thick and his hair so black, Berryman looks fierce from the back. Face-on it's different. People trust him right away. Nearly everyone does.

Thomas Berryman says he's a hard worker, a brooder when it comes to work. He says he'd read all of Charles Dickens by the time he was fourteen, but that he just did it to accomplish a task.

He's a broad-shouldered man, with beautiful woolly hair, and a seemingly darker, bushy, Civil War mustache.

His look reminded me of Irish football players, or at least my limited sports-desk experience with their pictures. Also, he would be right for Tiparillo cigar ads.

On this particular June morning, he flicked on a Carousel projector's fan and tugged on a customary wake-up cigar.

He pulled curtains on a full wall of glass, and Central Park's lollipop trees and hansom cabs disappeared. The Plaza Hotel disappeared.

One lazy-bodied horse in a blue straw hat disappeared last and caused Berryman to laugh. He hadn't worked for four months. He'd played in the sun at Mazatlán and Caneel Bay. He was fresh as a rose.

Thomas Berryman sometimes spoke of his individual jobs as numbers. He would talk about getting ready for another little number; about having performed a number. In that respect, this would be the Horn number.

For the next three days he arduously prepared for his meeting with Jimmie Lee Horn. He read everything ever written about Horn, and everything Horn himself had written. He read everything that was available, twice. Until his eyes began to hurt. Until his brain wore raw.

Sitting in his cramped library, he was thorough as an archbishop's secretary, wore no cowboy boots, wore high-priced cologne, read Larry McMurtry books to relax. Thomas Berryman's *idée fixe* was to *study, study, study*, and then *study* some more.

• • •

Life with Berryman had been good to Ben Toy.

He lived in a six-hundred-and-ninety-five-dollar-a-month penthouse. He owned and occasionally operated the Flower & Toy Shop on East 89th Street in Yorkville. The tiny florist shop was his hobby. Something he felt made him more than just a wiseass cowboy with a few dollars to throw around in bars.

One afternoon as he was locking up the shop—his free arm was holding a leather satchel; his cigarette was tilted up at a rakish angle—he was very suddenly drained of every ounce of cool, or bourgeois chic, or whatever it is that currently describes the Upper East Side demeanor.

Toy thought he had seen Harley Wynn watching him from the corner of East End Avenue.

First Toy squinted down the street into the sun. Then he started to jog, his handbag making him look slightly feminine in spite of his bulk.

Wynn—whoever it was—turned to light a cigarette out of the wind. Very Alfred Hitchcock. Then he disappeared into the chimney-red brownstone on the corner.

Toy ran up and stopped on the sidewalk in front of the house. He started to call out. "Wynn," he shouted huskily. Up to the rooftops.

"Wynn! Yo! Hey Wynn. Hey you fucking asshole!" he shouted. "Hey, you!"

There were lots of blue and red flowerpots in the windows on the top floor. No lights on the second floor. No Wynn.

A little old woman in a whorehouse-red kimono came out on her terrace to look at him. Big dogs inside the house started barking. Doormen were peering down the street like the town gossips they were.

Ben Toy finally hailed a yellow cab dawdling on the side street. He took it over to the West Side. He popped a Stelazine tablet en route, and consequently forgot to tell Berryman about the man who looked like Harley John Wynn.

•   •   •

I bent over closer to Ben Toy. Either the mattress or his pajamas smelled of urine. "Harley Wynn," I said.

His eyes popped open. They were blue. He'd been on the verge of falling asleep.

"Thorazine." He licked dry, chapped lips. "Makes you sleepy as hell."

"Just a few more questions," I said. "A couple of important ones."

Toy sighed. Then he nodded.

"Was Harley Wynn definitely a southerner?" I asked.

"Sure." Toy curled up on the end of the bare mattress. He shivered. "Just as much as you are . . . Could I have a blanket?" He asked Asher in a sweet, boyish voice. It was a strange sound coming out of a big man with two days' stubble on his chin.

"Answer his questions," the aide told him. "You know you can have a blanket, Ben. So just cut the crap, all right?"

"Can I have a blanket *now?*"

Asher pointed at me. He lighted up his pipe and stared out the window into blackness.

Toy struggled upright and sat with his bare back against the plaster wall. He was starting to pout, I thought. I hoped the aide knew what he was doing.

"Do you know where Wynn came from?" I asked.

Toy's answer was curt. "Tennessee."

"Are you sure?"

"I *said* Tennessee didn't I."

I was starting to feel guilty about grilling him too much. "OK, I'm sorry," I said. "I only have one more question, Ben."

"Shoot, *Ochs*."

"I'm not trying to condescend to you. I'm really not."

Toy smiled as though we were only playing a little game anyway. A lot of Joe Buck Conneroo came through with the smile.

"You said that Wynn wasn't hiring you himself . . ."

"No. He was a front man. Always said, 'They said' this; 'They said' that. He was a small fish. Just like me."

"OK then, do you know who hired Berryman?"

Ben Toy looked over at Asher, then at me. "Can't say."

My palm came down hard on the floor. "We've come a long ways tonight to start that shit now," I said.

"I really don't know," Toy said then. "I never knew who it was. Berryman knew."

Toy closed his eyes for a full two or three minutes after that answer.

Asher and I sat in total, eerie silence, just watching him breathe. The young aide had a dazed, tired look on his face. I figured I was probably pop-eyed myself.

Toy licked his chapped lips again. He shivered as though he were dropping off to sleep.

Rock and roll erupted in a nearby room and his eyes popped open again. He seemed annoyed that we were still in his room. Annoyed and slightly wild-eyed.

"Can I go to sleep now?" The soft, southern voice again. "Would you turn on the dimmer, please?"

"I'll talk tomorrow if you want." He turned to me.

For no reason I can imagine now, I reached over and shook Ben Toy's hand. I wished him good night.

Maybe the reason was that our first interview had completely caved in my mind . . . Right from when Toy had begun to describe the money transfer in Provincetown, I'd known I had a big story.

• • •

Walking beside Ronald Asher, coming down the hallway from the quiet room, I flashed a bad scene I'd been part of five days earlier at the *Citizen-Reporter* offices.

A copy cub, an arrogant nineteen-year-old black, had come up to my desk and sat down all over my paperwork that afternoon. The young writer's name was John Seawright, and he was in the habit of riding me about verisimilitude in my Horn articles. I was just about to tell him to get off the desk, and out of my life, when he grabbed hold of my shoulders and began to cry. "They just shot him," he sobbed. "They shot Jimmie Horn, man. He's dead," the boy told me. That was how I'd found out about Horn. Zap.

Someone somewhere on the hospital ward was playing an out-of-tune piano. "A House Is Not a Home" was the song.

I was still fairly shell-shocked from the interview.

The high yellow corridor lights were turned down low. It made it difficult for me not to peek into the brighter bedrooms we were passing.

Two middle-aged men who appeared to be twins were playing chess in one room.

A boy in his underwear was sitting in bed reading a mathematics text in another.

A young boy in hornrims was reading *Shockproof Sydney Skate* by Marijane Meaker.

I looked down at Asher. *The Beard*. There was something about the scraggly face growth that appealed to me.

"I've been thinking about a beard." I broke our mutual silence. "I don't understand my motivation though."

"You want people to know how smart you really are," the aide grinned. "Beard's a pain-in-the-ass way to do it though. Always getting spaghetti and cake in mine."

"I don't want people to think I'm smart." I watched the dull ceiling lights pass over my head. "I don't know exactly what it is. Not that, though."

We stopped at the patients' kitchen and he went on about the physical hardships of a beard. It was the kind of conversation people have at wakes down South—you talk about anything but the wake and the wakee.

Asher poured out some of the blackest coffee I'd ever seen. He had kind of an intriguing job, I was thinking.

I was also watching a pimply teenager who was in the kitchen with us. The boy was shoveling tablespoons of sugar into a tall glass of milk. He had fuzzy, electric hair and looked burned out at sixteen.

A fairly good (pragmatic) idea occurred to me in the kitchen. I began building up the nerve to ask Asher for an important favor.

"How much do you know about all this?" I asked for starters.

"The whole." Asher sipped the black coffee. "Just about, anyway. Shulman took me to dinner tonight. He told me the *hospital* position. He said I'd be the only one to supervise visits between you and Ben."

I put cream and raw sugar in my coffee. All motions. I wasn't going to drink the muddy geedunk. It reminded me of the Mississippi River.

"So you're pretty tight with Shulman?"

"We agree. We disagree. He generalizes too much for my taste. Textbooks sometimes. Basically he trusts my instincts, though. Believe it or not, I was in Columbia before this."

"He told you about Jimmie Horn?" I said.

"Yes, he told me. But I still wasn't prepared for what I heard back there with Toy. Most of us hadn't taken him all that seriously before."

I decided to ask Asher for a big favor. I was close to blurting it out anyway.

I started by moronically sipping some coffee.

"I don't want to play on your emotions," I said, "but I knew Horn for about eight years before this happened.

"In a lot of ways we were friends. In *some* ways," I corrected myself. "That doesn't have anything to do with you . . . except that it gives you an idea of what's going on in my head right now. My mind is a fucking wreck."

The aide nodded. Once again, the coffee.

"OK," I sighed. "*The problem* . . . I'd like to read what's been written about Toy since he's been in here . . . I could ask Alan Shulman. But I'm afraid to. If Shulman turns me down, I'm fucked. I'm looking for names, dates, anything about Thomas Berryman. I swear to you that I won't use anything that would hurt anybody else in here. On Bowditch."

Asher nodded again. He really looked exhausted and I felt sorry for him. His eyes shifted out the kitchen window into the dark exercise yard.

Beyond the floodlights on the wall was a staff parking lot. Then the end of the hospital grounds. Then the ocean. At night you could only see the wall, though. Salvador Dali couldn't have done it better.

"When you turn left outside the front door, the inside door," Asher turned to me, "there's a small conference room. Wait in there. I'll try to get you what you need."

The aide brought me Ben Toy's admission notes, workup notes, daily nursing charts—over two hundred pages in all.

Everything was stamped CONFIDENTIAL or NOT TO BE REMOVED FROM THIS ROOM. Some of it was typed, but most of the notes were handwritten in black ink.

I started to copy names, addresses, telephone numbers . . .

Jimmie Horn was mentioned several times in the daily notes; Harley Wynn was mentioned; Thomas Berryman didn't come up that frequently.

I recognized none of the other names or addresses. There was nothing to immediately connect anyone in Tennessee.

I found Toy's admission note especially interesting though:

> Mr. Toy is an extremely handsome, well-developed young man from the northwestern part of Texas. He has a history of not having close, stable relationships, with the exception of one longstanding boyhood relationship.
> Mr. Toy claims to have killed a man and a woman, and some traumatic incident has precipitated a severe depression with accompanying physical hostility. (He punches walls and people.)
> Mr. Toy has also had auditory hallucinations. Immediate care inside a psychiatric hospital is recommended, and suicidal behavior should not be discounted with this young man . . .

I stopped reading as I remembered one fact that put a damper on my excitement and speculation about Toy and Thomas Berryman. Jimmie Horn had been shot down by Bert Poole. I'd seen it several times on film. It was as clear in my mind as the famous televised sequence in which Jack Ruby shot Lee Harvey Oswald.

• • •

Bowditch was silent around me, reminding me of late nights in my own house. The only sound was water running through the old building's pipes. Then it *glug-glugged* off. It was 2:30 in the morning. I was feeling ever so slightly deranged.

I sat with my stockinged feet up on a green-blottered desk, smoking, drinking machine coffee, thinking about both Ben Toy and Ronald Asher.

I knew I had a story now, probably a pretty good one, and I started to consider more thorough approaches for future interviews.

I knew from past experience that I should quickly identify myself and my newspaper. People like to have situations with strangers defined . . . Then, I thought it would be best to work off people's natural sympathies for Jimmie Horn. For political assassinations anyway.

I scribbled out a speech for myself, but it was so convoluted people would have forgotten the beginning by the time I reached the end.

Then I considered a very simple, direct approach.

"My name is Ochs Jones," it went. "I'm a reporter for the *Nashville Citizen-Reporter* (local newspaper if necessary). I'm investigating the murder of Jimmie Horn of Nashville. Would you help me?"

It was an introduction that never failed me during four months of investigation, in six states.

Watching out for the inevitable attendant or security guard, I let myself out Bowditch's unlocked outside door. (There were three doors; two of them were locked, but the one leading into the foyer wasn't.)

Alan Shulman was waiting for me, sitting on the front steps.

The young doctor was dressed in well-worn sixties street clothes; he was scratching little xs and os in the driveway gravel with two-toned desert boots.

"Asher called you," I said.

He nodded. "I wish you'd asked me for those flies," he said. "That really bothers me, Mr. Jones."

Then he got up from the front steps and walked inside. I listened to the two inner doors being unlocked, closed. Then it was silent again.

I wished I'd asked him too.

I also wished he hadn't dealt with it in quite that way.

West Hampton, July 10

For breakfast the next morning I sat alone in a wrinkled double bed at Howard Johnson's and tried to write the first news story about Thomas Berryman. I didn't do spectacularly well.

Random Observation: We of the new journalism schools, *energetic, smarter than anybody else, insane with the desire to say truths*—simply cannot express ourselves as well as many of our elders.

Random Observation: People I know, kith and kin, like to compare newspaper and police investigation to jigsaw puzzle solving ... but if the investigations I've worked on are anything like the average jigsaw puzzle—it's a puzzle where all the pieces have been lost.

Lost in different places. Around the house, the backyard, the car, anywhere the car may have been since the puzzle was bought.

Before a reporter can try to put the puzzle together, he has to find all the pieces.

I sat in the motel bed looking at all of my pieces. Exposés are made of this:

> The name of a bar in Provincetown, Mass.: A. J. Fogarty's.
> A hotel: the Bay Arms (also in Provincetown).
> A New York florist's: Flower & Toy Shop.

Phone numbers Ben Toy had charged calls to since entering the hospital:

> 212-686-4212 (Carole Ann Mahoney)
> 312-238-1774 (Robert Stringer)
> 617-753-8581 (Bernard Shaw)
> 212-838-6643 (Mary Ellen Terry)

212-259-9311 (Berryman; N.Y.C.)
516-249-6835 (Berryman; Long Island)

Names: Dr. Reva Baumwell (100 Park); Michel Romains; Charles Izzie; Ina and Calvin Toy.

I added notes to myself:

> Call Lewis Rosten (my editor) about gunman in Philadelphia.
> Call Alan Shulman about lunch and/or boxing match.

I called N.Y. telephone information and asked for the number of Thomas Berryman in Manhattan.

They gave me 259-9311, which I knew of course.

"That's at 60 West 80th Street?" I then asked.

"No, sir," the operator said. "It's 80 Central Park South."

I added Berryman's New York address to my list.

Then I started dialing the other numbers.

The response at 686-4212 set the tone for the rest of my morning. A young woman with a bright, friendly, mid-western voice answered.

"Hi there."

"Hi. My name is Ochs Jones. I'm a friend of Ben Toy's."

"Who?"

"Ben Toy, Thomas Berryman . . . They said that you . . ."

"Oh. Hold on. You must want Maggie."

Off receiver: "Mags, a friend of Ben Toy? . . ."

The phone is set down on a table. Sounds of women walking around in high heels on hardwood floors. Ten minutes pass. The phone is hung up. I call again and there's no answer.

The desk at the Bay Arms Hotel in Provincetown had no record of a Toy or Berryman staying there during the month of June.

A. J. Fogarty's suggested I call after five, when the night staff came on.

There was no answer at the florist's.

Both Hertz and Avis said there was no way Harley Wynn or anyone else could have rented a Lincoln Mark IV at Boston's Logan Airport. The Wizard at Avis said it was a "logistical impossibility."

Around noon I decided to call Lewis Rosten. Lewis is my editor at the *Citizen-Reporter*. He's a thick-skinned wordsmith out of the University of the South—Sewanee. He's 100% bite, no bark, and the prime mover behind this book. Also, he's my friend.

It sounded like he'd just arrived at the office.

"Ochs, how is it going? Or isn't it? Where are you?"

"Still up on Long Island," I said. "You sound pretty chipper. Must have a pretty good headline going for today."

"It's pure rubbish." Rosten drawled pure Mississippi. "Speculation about this Joe Cubbah cat up in Philadelphia."

"I talked with Ben Toy at the hospital last night," I said. "I really think this might be something, Lewis."

I read from my notes on Toy, filling in my own gut feelings.

"Jeeee-ssus!" Rosten yowled when I was finished. "I was going to apologize for sending you up there in the middle of things down here . . . I just had this feeling about that doctor who called . . . Listen," Rosten said, "Toy said, '*I can't tell you*,' when you first asked him who had hired Thomas Berryman?"

"Yeah. But then he came right back and said he didn't know. It's hard to read Toy. They have him on a ton of medication . . . Apparently he's kicked the shit out of some attendants. He's a pretty big boy."

"How did they get him in there anyway?"

"You know, I don't know . . . I don't have all the details anyway. He fell asleep on me last night."

Rosten wasn't too happy with that one.

"When do you see him again?" he wanted to know.

"I hope today . . . I, uh, made a few problems for myself last night. Looked at some hospital workups on Toy. Got caught."

Far, far away in Nashville Rosten calmly puffed away on his pipe. "Accidents," he muttered, "will occur in the best-regulated families. Mister Charles Dickens, *David Copperfield* . . . Ochs," he went on in the same breath, "please be careful with this."

I sat at the motel desk and smoked a few more cigarettes. It was bright noon outside.

Some little girls were having a high-diving marathon in the swimming pool.

I went back over what I had and what I didn't have point by point. Among other things, it occurred to me that I had absolutely no idea how or why the gunman from Philadelphia had been in Nashville. Not a clue.

It also occurred to me that I had no idea what had happened to Thomas Berryman. I sat there, puffing tobacco, watching little girls play, wondering where Berryman was right at that very moment.

West Hampton, July 11

Two husky attendants were wrapping Ben Toy up like Tutankhamen, only in wet, ice-cold sheets. He lay flat out on one of two pinewood massage tables in the immaculate Bowditch shower room.

One aide pulled the dripping sheets tight, then the other held them down—the way you'd keep a finger on string while wrapping a package.

The tightly bound sheets trapped all of Toy's body heat; made it numb; floated his mind. He started to look like he was knocked out on dope.

As we sat in the shower room, different smart-aleck patients kept coming in and threatening to sit on his face. That was a big joke on Bowditch. The intruders always laughed; Ben Toy laughed.

There was a strange camaraderie among the patients that wouldn't have held up on the outside. It was disorienting, but I was "being careful" as per Lewis Rosten's request. This was meeting number 2, and Toy had requested "cold packs" for it.

I bent down and touched a Winston to his chapped lips. His face pores were open, exuding oily sweat.

He drew smoke slowly, deep, then exhaled it in a steamy cloud. There was something expensive, exotic, about the entire experience, the madhouse atmosphere.

"It really relaxes me," Toy said of the cold packs. His drawn cheeks and his forehead were starting to flush bright red. "You fight like a bastard the first time they try to do it to you. Then you can't get enough of it."

He exhaled more smoke. He tried to blow it up to the green tile ceiling.

My eyes traveled up and down the neatly bound-up sheets. I looked over at Asher. He and I had squared things with Shulman. Kind of squared things, anyway. "I think I'd put up a little fight if you tried to put me in these, " I said.

Toy smiled. His eyes were on the Winston in my hand. "One more puff," he said. "Then I have a story for you."

The story elaborated on Thomas Berryman's unconventional techniques for murder.

The most recent *number* had occurred in the small town of Lake Stevens, Washington. The victims were two of three brothers owning an airplane company: Shepherd Industries of Washington.

Berryman was used because the deaths had to appear accidental; suspicion had to be cast away from the family: the man paying Berryman's forty thousand dollar fee was the third brother.

I recalled Harley Wynn's remarks about displacing blame after the murder of Jimmie Horn. If Berryman had somehow done the shooting in Nashville, he certainly had succeeded in that regard.

The Shepherd Number had taken him three days to complete.

On January 17th, a Friday, he'd flown to the Shepherd family estate in Lake Stevens. He was posed as a sales representative for a Michigan tool and die company, Michael J. Shear. On Monday, he and all three brothers were scheduled to go to Detroit to inspect Shear's plant operations.

Berryman's plan for the job was characteristically complicated in execution. It unraveled, however, with a fascinating, what Ben Toy called a "neat," result.

As I listened I considered the related parallels for Jimmie Horn.

Lake Stevens, Washington, January 19 and 20

On a Sunday night, the 19th of January, Thomas Berryman sat in a moonlit kitchen, lazily drinking instant coffee, daydreaming about a girl named Oona Quinn.

He listened for noises around him in the big Shepherd house. Heard the cold wind in the firs outside. The soothing fire crackling under his water pan.

A plastic clock on the stove read five of two.

At two, Berryman pushed himself back from the table. He held back a yawn and pinched grit out of the corners of his eyes. He went outside into the winter cold.

The night air was better for his concentration. Still, he felt that he was sleepwalking for a while.

He was carrying a duffel bag the size of a lunchbox. Also an oversized pistol, a five-inch Crossman air pistol.

His tennis shoes made a padding sound across the patio. Then he was stiff-arming tree and bush forms in the dark.

Following a skinny, winding creek that carried the moon's reflection like a boat, Berryman was eventually turning a dogleg right in the woods. In time he saw amber floodlights from the Shepherd airfield. Saw how they seemed to pin down the planes like guy wires.

Down under one plane's nose an old Chevy BelAir was parked alongside a slender clapboard sentry house. Berryman could read I BRAKE FOR ANIMALS on a big orange sticker across the car's trunk. Farmers with night jobs, he considered. Maybe down-and-outers.

A hairy gray head was in one sentry house window. A muffled radio played country and western music. Charlie Pride, it sounded like.

About a quarter mile down the field he could see the jet he'd come in on that past Friday. Staying about ten feet inside the woods, he made a way, the long way, down toward the jet.

He noticed several lean Dobermans roaming loose, prancing on the shiny tarmac, apparently liking the sound made by their paws on stone.

Out beyond the main lights the field got dark enough for Berryman to walk out of the bushes again. Far down the airfield, a younger guard came up to the little pillbox with a leashed Doberman. He tied up the muscular animal, and for a minute or two it stood around front snapping at its old lady, also tied.

As Berryman stood watching the pair, a hidden Doberman flew out of the tree shadows. It barked no warning, growled late.

Berryman fell, and the long Crossman flashed up with an airy *pffssss. Pffssss*. The pretty dog twisted around itself and collapsed. It lay still with its teeth bared, the way dogs look after they've tried, too late, to bite killer automobiles.

The Doberman would sleep for hours. Then, it would wake up yipping and limping. With religion.

The younger of the two watchmen wasn't going to be so fortunate. Berryman needed him.

He pushed himself up from the cold airfield tarmac. Felt where his coat and sweater were ripped at the elbow. He started off toward the jet, and a long night's work.

The following morning, Berryman prowled around the Shepherd kitchen like a sick man. He had butterflies in his stomach and he was trembling slightly. Among other things, he hadn't slept that night.

Across the room, a little blacklady cook was doing a slow burn.

Morality had never been ambiguous with the woman and she highly disapproved of a party held there the night before. She held Thomas Berryman responsible.

He'd arranged the bash.

"Hmmpff. I jus won't work 'round here no more, things being like this," she complained around the kitchen. "Hmmpff."

She scrambled a bowl of eggs and kept shaking her head in disgust. "Women's underwears in the garden. Little maraschinos cherries in the swimmin' pool. Hmmpff. Hmmpff." She turned to Berryman and looked him squarely in the face: wise little acorn face to big mustache face. "I thought you was a gentleman," she said. "Wrong. Wrong again," she shrugged. "Won't be the first time. Won't be the last."

Berryman was fiddling over by her stove, looking half-contrite. He appeared to be sorry to have caused her displeasure, if nothing else. "What's this here?" he asked after a respectful pause.

"Hmmpff," the old lady bit her tongue. She beat her duck eggs dark gold. "Now what . . ." she said, biting the tongue, "now what in the world does that *look* like?"

Thomas Berryman cocked his head back and popped a biscuit-sized fruit into his mouth. "Tastes like strawberries," he grinned. "Only they're too big to be strawberries." Juice ran over his chin and he dammed the flow with a forefinger.

The cook moved over and nudged him away from her stove. She was half-playing now. "I'm really mad at you, Mister Shear."

She sidled him across the kitchen with her bony little hip. "You a bad influence comin up Lake Steven actin like that last night."

As further appeasement, it seemed, Berryman started to fill a row of four pewter coffee mugs on the counter. "Who's who?"

"Mister Ben an' you the cream an' sugar boys," the old lady started. Then she reconsidered. "But you not bringin nothin' to nobody. You must make it a big joke. Bit joke on Mrs. Bibbs, ha ha, very funny indeed."

"Put down the coffee," she said. "*Down* boy."

As the little black woman returned to scooping eggs onto warmed, waiting plates, Berryman dropped small tablets into two of the coffee mugs. The tablets were a combination of iron sulfate, magnesium oxide, and ipecac.

"What a sore sport," he sucked his cheek as he watched the pills dissolve. "What a party pooper, Mrs. B."

As he continued to grin at her, the old woman finally looked up. She flashed a gold bridgework smile at him. As usual, he was forgiven.

The youngest Shepherd brother, Benjamin, sat still as grass, glassy-eyed, chewing a breakfast muffin over and over like it was rubber tire. He thought he was having a heart attack.

He could hear his big heart thumping and felt it could blow open his chest. His body was flushing blood. Numb fingers, toes. His lungs were filling up with fluids, and he was having regrets about the life he'd led.

Pancakes were being passed by. His brother was kidding Thomas Berryman about the trip back to Michigan.

Benjamin Shepherd slipped down to the floor, and began vomiting recognizable food.

Charles and William Shepherd carried their brother to a first floor bedroom. They held him on a bed while his body convulsed. He dryheaved. His back arched like a drawbridge.

Gradually it dawned on Charles Shepherd that his cook was screaming bloody murder in another room. Back in the dining room. She screamed for a long time, calling for Charles Shepherd and for Jesus.

When his young brother finally fainted, Charles ran back to the dining room.

What he found was Thomas Berryman lying across the rug. Berryman was holding his knees up around his chest. He'd kicked over the dining room table—at least it was turned over on its side. "Oh my God," he kept gasping. "Oh God, it's horrible." He wasn't having regrets about the life he'd led. He'd poisoned himself.

The exact sound he made was: O g-a-a-ad.

• • •

Late that afternoon the little cook, Mrs. Bibbs, sat on a tiny leather hassock in the front hallway of the Shepherd house. She'd cried until she had no control over her limbs. The sun was passing down through the glass portion of the front door. The woman slipped off the hassock onto the sunstreaked floor.

The family doctor had just gone out the door. He'd said that both Berryman and Benjamin Shepherd had suffered from acute food poisoning. It was lucky for them, he announced with great pomp, that they'd both thrown up so violently.

Orating in front of Charles and Willy Shepherd, the doctor had sternly and ridiculously questioned the cook about whether or not she'd washed her strawberries before serving them. "I think not," he'd said. And who was she to argue with a doctor of medicine.

That afternoon, Benjamin Shepherd was recuperating in his own bedroom.

Propped in front of a Trinitron portable, eating ice cream like a tonsillectomy patient, his large head was positioned beneath a framed Kodachrome of Maria Schneider in *Last Tango in Paris*. The girl had more hair over her vagina than an ape does.

Benjamin wasn't flying back to Michigan with Berryman and his brothers, he'd announced.

The family advised Thomas Berryman to do the same. Recuperate for a few days. Get the poisons out of his system. Take rhubarb and soda at regular intervals.

But when Charles and Willy Shepherd stopped to see their brother on their way to the plane, Berryman, though peaked, was packed and dressed to travel with them.

He was smiling thinly. Puffing on a characteristic cigarillo. But he looked like a man just over a hospital convalescence.

That much is approximated in a statement filed by Ben Shepherd with the Lake Stevens, Washington, police.

Pioneer types, Charles and Willy Shepherd fueled and set up their own plane. It was work they liked doing.

Berryman pitched in where he could, driving a BP fuel truck back and forth from a hangar. The three men worked without speaking.

It wasn't until all the work was done that Berryman took Charles Shepherd aside.

They sat down on a small metal handtruck beside the private jet's boarding stairs. Berryman was hyperventilating. Charles Shepherd's hands were dirty as a mechanic's and he sat with them held out away from his shirt.

"Whew!" Berryman kept blowing out air and catching his breath as he spoke. "I guess," he said, "all this *phew* extra running around . . . set me off again."

"Sure it did," Shepherd agreed. "You should be back in bed. You look pitiful."

"Damn stomach's rolling."

"Rhubarb and soda's the thing."

"Fuck me," Berryman puffed.

"I told you, you dumbass. Go on back with Ben now."

Thomas Berryman continued to swear like a man about to miss out on box seats for a pro football game. "Shee-it," he said over and over.

Willy Shepherd stood close by, looking as if he'd suddenly figured something out. He was lighting a cigarette "Too much running around," he said to Berryman. "Got to take it easy after these things."

"Phew," Berryman said. He was beet red, blushing "Fuck me, Willy" were his last words, really, to either of the brothers. He gave both men back-thumping *abrazos* Then he headed back toward the big house.

•   •   •

The private plane cruised over Douglas fir tops like a living, looking thing. It was blue, electric blue.

Thomas Berryman watched through mottled leaves that were hiding his face. Then he turned away and began hiking through woods toward the main state road, away from the house.

Berryman walked watching the tops of his boots Watching the underbrush. The bleached hay. Noting greenish grasshoppers. Red ants on stalks of hay. A dead field mouse like a wet, gray mitten.

Overhead, the blue jet's wheels slowly tucked into its stomach, and as the wheels folded, the sky cracked like a giant fir splitting all the way up from its roots.

Berryman knew enough not to look back. Once, sometime in Texas, he'd seen a buck on fire. It hadn't been pretty, or edifying.

He walked faster. In deeper woods. In a dark house with a soft needle floor. He kept seeing the burning deer.

The nose and the belly puffed smoke just about the color of sheep wool. It shot flames that were orange at first. Then just about blue. Then near-invisible in black smoke.

It smoked ashes. It made shrieking metal-against-metal noises. The entire dark sky seemed to fall into the woods.

That much was reported by a gas station owner on the Lake Stevens Highway.

Berryman hiked two miles to a picnic roadstop. The road-stop was simply two redwood tables in a small clearing.

He got into a rented beige and white camper he'd parked there earlier in the week.

There were sleeping bags and Garcia fishing poles and tackle in the back. There was a Texaco map of Washington across the front seat. An old pipe was on the dashboard.

Propped against the pipe was the familiar old sign: GONE-FISHING. Berryman crumpled the message in his hand.

He turned on the radio. Opened all the windows. Put on a workshirt, Stetson, and Tony Lama boots. He drove away calmly, like a man away on a vacation.

The smell of fir was so thick and good he began to get over his nausea from the ipecac residue.

Hours later, sitting in a roadhouse in Cahone, Oregon, he read that businessman Michael J. Shear (the body of the young airfield security guard) was among those killed in the crash of a private plane near the Charles Shepherd estate in Lake Stevens, Washington. There wasn't any mention of an investigation, the local media aura being one of either supernatural catastrophe, or casual indifference. (Even afterward, the matter of the missing security guard was either overlooked or attributed to coincidence by the tiny Lake Stevens police force.)

There was an accompanying photograph with the newspaper story. It showed a sad and silly-looking policeman holding up a large man's shoe.

Because he had extended it out toward the camera, it looked like a giant's shoe. This was the same trick used in "big fish" photos, and Berryman wondered if the man had done it on purpose.

• • •

Ben Toy lay still as a corpse in his cold packs. His blond hair was wet, darker. I'd pushed it back out of his face, and he looked younger that way.

"That's the way his mind works," he said to me, to Asher and the Sony.

"And that's why they wanted him for Jimmie Horn."

New York City, July 12

At 9:30 the next morning I was perched on a four-foot-high stone wall surrounding Central Park. I was memorizing Thomas Berryman's apartment building as though it was Westminster Abbey or the Louvre.

My hands had been sweating when I woke up at 6 A.M.;

they were still sweating. I'd been considering calling the police. The blood-and-shit terribleness of the story was just beginning to dawn on me and it was oppressive.

I had a good idea what I was going to do at Berryman's, only not knowing New York, I didn't think it would be quite as easy as it turned out to be.

Between nine-thirty and ten, two liveried doormen whistled down Yellow Cab after Yellow Cab in front of the building. It's gray-canopied entrance, marked with a big white number 80, seemed a glorified bus stop more than anything else.

My hands continued to sweat. Even my legs were wet. For sharp contrast I could see suits and jewels munching breakfast across the way at the Park Lane Hotel.

Ben Toy had spoken of the tenth floor . . . dirty ledges . . . pigeons. I counted up to the tenth floor. But there were no pigeons that day; and no people at any of the windows. The windows appeared to be black.

After the taxi rush, one of the doormen emerged from the lobby trailing four large dogs on leashes. A dapper blackman in his forties, he was wearing a dark green suitcoat over his blue uniform—that plus a race-track fedora with a little yellow feather cocked up on the side.

He controlled the dogs with flicks of his wrists, getting them to successfully jaywalk through Central Park South's midmorning traffic.

I caught up with him on a secluded patch of lawn inside

the park. It was under the eye of RCA and GM; of planted penthouse terraces and wooden water towers. I told the doorman my name and business, and he was sympathetic, I thought. He'd been born in Kentucky, in fact, and he knew about Horn. His name was Leroy Bones Cooper.

"Well, sure, yes, I'd like to cooperate with you on this matter of Mr. Horn," he said without any southern in his voice. "I didn't person'ly know the man, you understand—I believe I did see him on the news program several times."

I quickly decided to ask the doorman if he could possibly get me inside Berryman's apartment.

His reaction was sudden inner-city suspicion. "Mr. Berr'man?" He cocked his head on a sharp slant. "What does Mr. Berr'man have to do with it? He been away lately."

"He might not be involved at all," I told the man. "We think he is, though."

The doorman started to lead his dogs back toward the street. "Hard for me to believe that," he said over their sudden barking.

I trailed along, about a step behind. "Can I ask why?"

The little blackman seemed a little angry now. "You askin it," he said. He took off his hat and wiped his head with a big white hankie. "Don't have no answer for sure." He looked at me. "Mr. Berr'man's a nice young fella is all. Stock man or manageer'ial I believe."

He continued to walk forward. The dogs were being irritated by squirrels in the maple trees.

"The way I see it," he turned to me when we reached

the stone wall, "it's twenty-five dollars for me. Twenty-five for the super."

I didn't quite believe what he'd said. I brought up the concern he'd shown about Horn.

"Whether I'm concerned or whether I'm not," he waved off my objection, "you want your peek upstairs. The money's its own separate thing. I see how it can help Mr. Horn, all right, and it can help me too."

I let the argument drop and I counted out five ten-dollar bills for Cooper. He thanked me in a polite, New York-doorman way. He wasn't from Kentucky, I thought—not anymore.

"You're going to take me up there yourself," I told the little man.

• • •

Leroy Cooper was making a lot of throat-clearing and sniffling noises. He was having trouble unlocking the heavy green door marked with a gold 10D.

The strong-box door finally opened, and I was looking across a long room, all the way up Central Park to 110th Street. It was a spectacular view of bright woods, narrow roads, even a few dark ponds.

The apartment itself was weighted down with heavy wood furniture and hanging plants. It was conspicuously neat and clean.

"Maid comes two, three times a week. Ears'la Libscomb," Cooper said. "Anybody else comes," he cautioned me with a stiff outstretched finger, *"you're* a burglar."

"Thanks," I mumbled. "I thought I might be able to count on you."

"I hope you find what you're looking for," he said anyway. His knobby, black hands were visibly shaking, but he was trying to look arrogant. He was totally confused, I decided.

He slowly, noiselessly closed the door and I was alone in Thomas Berryman's apartment.

Feeling more than a little unreal, I set right to work. I started with a quick tour of the place.

Besides the airy living room, there were two large bedrooms. There was an eat-in kitchen and another large room being used as a study. I walked along flinging open closets, pulling out drawers, making quite an arbitrary mess of things.

I found a Walther automatic in the master bedroom, but there were no other guns anywhere.

There were photographs of an exquisite, dark-haired girl over a fireplace in the bedroom. She was an Irisher ... There were also black-and-white photographs and paintings of *Last Picture Show* western towns all over the walls. But there were no pictures of Thomas Berryman.

Only clues about him.

Blouses and Cardin and Yves Saint Laurent suits next to hunting wear from Abercrombie's. Boots from Neiman-Marcus. Givenchy colognes. A rugged-looking jacket made of the good, soft leather used for horse equipage.

The second bedroom seemed to be some kind of guest room with bath.

It was all set up like a room at the Plaza Hotel. Fresh untouched Turkish towels and linen. Neutrogena soap still in its black wrapper. An unused tube of Close-up that I opened for candy purposes.

The study was full of books and cigars, and also one of the few things I'd specifically been looking for.

It was a fat, red book published by Random House. The maid or someone had put it upside down on one of the bookshelves. The book was called *Jiminy* and it was Jimmie Horn's autobiography.

Close beside *Jiminy* were four other books containing articles on Horn: *Sambo; The Young Bloods; Black Consciousness*; and *Re-Nig*.

My next interesting discovery was three photographs. They were wrapped up in tissue paper and squirreled away in a bottom desk drawer.

One of them showed a well-dressed blond man who seemed to be signaling for a cab on a crowded, glittery street. The blond man was in crisp, sharp focus.

The second picture was of the same blond man turned toward a street hustler this time. The second man wore blue-jean biballs with no shirt, and a bluejean cap with a peak. The blond man's eyes were half-closed and his mouth was open in a capital O. It looked like a candid comedy picture.

The final shot was the blond man again, but standing beside Ben Toy. This Ben Toy weighed twenty to thirty pounds more than when I'd seen him at the hospital. He was physically impressive to look at. Behind the two men was a white municipal building, a library or courthouse. The blond man seemed to be pointing right at the camera.

I was certain that he was Harley John Wynn.

Soon after I looked at the pictures, I heard a loud creaking noise inside the apartment. I looked across the room, and saw that the front door was slowly opening. I was helpless to do anything but watch it.

First a hat, then Leroy Cooper's face appeared in a foot-wide crack. "How long you gonna be?" he complained. "Damn, man, you're taking too long for this."

I said nothing to Cooper. I felt as though my skull had been shattered by someone swinging a heavy metal bar. Somehow, the experience had translated into nausea too.

Getting no answer from me, Cooper slowly shook his head. He shut the door again. I heard him swearing outside. Very slowly, I was getting an emotional grasp of the situation I was involved in: I was starting to understand genuine fear of being hurt; the ability to take lives; fast, unexpected death.

Eventually I regrouped and left the building. I sent the three photographs to Lewis Rosten in Nashville. Then I spent the rest of the day visiting psychiatrists and psychologists who'd worked with Ben Toy.

I also ate a pork chop sandwich in a lunch shop run by some Greek men. The chop was silver-dollar size with the bone still in it. Because of the bone, the Greek men couldn't cut the sandwich. I ate around it, not completely understanding how or why people live in New York City.

That night, after dinner with Alan Shulman, I called home.

My wife Nan said she was missing me, and I was missing her too. Nan knows how to put me on an even keel, and I'd been flying just a little too high in New York.

We talked about the Berryman story, and talking with her I began to feel that I'd accomplished some things.

After we finished, Nan put on my daughters for two minutes each.

Janie Bug said almost nothing. Then she started to cry because her time was up.

Little Cat said she'd pray for me at Trinity Episcopal if I promised to bring her back one of those miniature Empire State Buildings.

That kind of thing (attitude) upsets me, but I don't know what to do about it.

I tried to go to sleep, but I couldn't quite get there.

Amagansett, July 13

Random Observation: I'd been handed a ticket on the fast rail, and I was well on my way to God knew where. It was Tom Wickerdom or bust.

Or was it? I began to remember strange, sad stories about men called "assassination buffs." I remembered people laughing at the expense of an ex-newsman from Memphis who was still dredging up facts about Martin Luther King's murder.

My body was trying to accept another northern morning. It was agreeably warm outside, but springwarm.

It was 8 A.M. and I was badly in need of a caffeine fix. I had to settle for nicotine, American-tobacco style.

Cigarette in hand, I surveyed a big, gray Victorian-style house bordering the yard of William Seward Junior High in Amagansett. I was fingering a rash under my new beard. In retrospect, I think the lack of sleep had caught up with me.

The big house had four white gables and a black Fleetwood sticking out of the garage. The house number told me it was Miss Ettie Hatfield's place, and I was properly impressed with the living style of the Bowditch nurse.

Miss Hatfield had been night charge nurse on Bowditch for over thirty-five years. Both Shulman and Ronald Asher said she was the only person on Bowditch Ben Toy might have opened up to. Miss Hatfield was a magical old lady, they said. She was the one who'd originally alerted Shulman to the Jimmie Horn references in Toy's ramblings.

I could distinguish a bald head reading a newspaper inside the house's darkened living room. Steam was drifting up from a coffee cup on the windowsill.

I slogged up the spongy-wet front lawn, stood on a wet, bristle mat, and tried to get a brass lionhead to make noise for me. The knocker would stick on the downswing—then it would make a sound like *ttthummm*. Stick, then *ttthummm*.

"Doesn't work right." A man's voice finally came from inside. "I'm coming around. I'm coming around."

He of the bald head, an ancient fellow in a plaid shirt with black string tie, finally opened up the front door.

He was Miss Hatfield's father, and he appeared to be well into his nineties. He shook from Parkinson's disease, he told me, but other than that, everything was shipshape.

"She's sleepin' now," he said after we'd gotten our autobiographies in order. "Works nights up the hospital. I just picked her up seven-fifteen."

The old man looked down at a handsome gold watch, searched the dial for arms, looked back up at me.

"Made my fortune sellin' these Benruses," he remarked. "You're about six foot six, aren't you?" he went on.

"Six foot seven," I blushed, then slouched out of an old, *no, I don't play basketball* habit.

Mr. Hatfield shook his head and made a clucking noise with his cheek. "Seventy-nine fuckin' inches," he said. "Here I stand sixty-one and a half. Used to be sixty-four. Hell, Ettie's near sixty-three herself."

I couldn't help laughing at the way he'd said it, and the old man chortled along with me. I asked what time I should come back to talk with his daughter.

"Aw hell, I'm goin' to wake her now."

He gave me a little hand signal to follow him inside. "She's been expectin' you all yesterday. Ever since Ben Toy told her you come. I ever let you get away, she'd cut me off my cream of wheat."

He went up the stairs chucking to himself. He was a country boy, in his own quaint Long Island, N.Y., way.

I met Miss Hatfield in a parlor room *already* smelling strongly of musk.

The nurse was a smily, white-haired lady with a little hitch in her walk. She was a fast-walking limper though, a female Walter Brennan.

"How're you this fine morning?" She shook my hand with some of the friendliness I'd been missing since coming up North. "I'm Ettie. Be more than happy to help you all I can . . . Alan Shulman already said it'd be fine." She grinned perfect shiny false teeth. "Heard about your mess-up with young Asher. Tsk. Tsk."

The little nurse had completely taken over the room. Her big smile was everywhere. Ettie shit, I was thinking, this was my Great-Aunt Mary Elizabeth Collins Jones—the one who had me pegged.

"Sit down. Sit down," she said to me. "Daddy, why don't you take a nice walk?" She turned to her father.

The old fellow had just settled into a cushiony velvet love seat. It took him a while to get up, and to hobble across the room. "Why don't she take a nice flyin' crap for herself?" he loud-whispered as he passed my chair.

"Not while this nice young man is here," Ettie Hatfield said without missing a beat.

She talked for as long as I wanted to listen. She was very thorough, very serious once she got going. She exhausted her memory for every last detail, cursing when one wouldn't come back to her.

The nurse had heard a lot of anecdotes about the way Ben Toy and Berryman had grown up in Texas; but she also knew stories about several of the killings. Curiosities, which I filled my notebook with:

Thomas Berryman had been married in Mexico when he was fifteen.

Berryman's mother died of lung cancer when he was eleven.

Both of them had apparently been well liked around Clyde, Texas. Berryman was called the "Pleasure King"; Ben Toy was called "the funniest man in America."

Ben Toy had gone through a period where he'd worn his mother's underwear whenever she left him alone in the house.

The first man Berryman ever shot was a priest from New Mexico.

Berryman had been wounded in a New York shooting in 1968.

Berryman had received one hundred thousand dollars in two payments to kill Jimmie Horn. The money was probably being held by a man named Michael Kittredge.

Ben Toy had advised Berryman not to take the Horn job. He didn't want to be party to the assassination. Berryman had told him Horn was going to be shot whether he did it or not.

"Most patients have their little tales," Miss Hatfield explained to me at one point. "You'll hear about how they've had relations with these three hundred women—and then they'll tell you how they think they may be impotent." The old lady laughed. "Sometimes it's not so funny. Sometimes it *is*, though.

"Now Ben Toy," she went on, "he was sounding pretty authentic to me. No attempt to impress anybody. No big contradictions in things he said ... That's why I told Doctor Shulman."

She stood up and stepped away from her easy chair. "I have something to show you," she said. "This is my big contribution."

She went over and got a brown schoolboy's duffel bag sitting beside the velvet love seat. "Carry all my little gewgaws to work in this," she laughed.

She unzippered the bag and reached around inside for a minute or so.

She took out a bent photograph and handed it over to me. Harley Wynn, I thought as I took it. But it was Berryman. The picture looked to be two or three years old, but it was definitely him. The curly black hair, the floppy mustache.

"It came in Ben Toy's things from his apartment," she said. "Kind of looks like a regular person, doesn't he? Some man you see anyday in Manhattan. That kind of frightens me." The old woman made a strange face by closing one eye tight. "I'd like to be able to look right at him and tell. Just by looking . . . like Lee Harvey Oswald. That one down in Alabama, too."

"Yeah." I agreed with what I thought she was saying. "And just like Bert Poole down in Tennessee," I added.

Nashville, July 14

My black swivel chair at the *Nashville Citizen-Reporter* is ancient. The line WHAT HAS HE DONE FOR US LATELY? is a recent addition to it, chalked across the back in three bold lines. Something about the chair makes me think of black leather jackets.

I sit under a gold four-sided clock hanging at the center of a huge two-hundred-foot-by-one-hundred-and-fifty-foot city room. I doubt that anything other than the people inside the room has changed since the 1930s.

At noon, only one other typewriter was going in the whole place. Most of the writers and editors would come in around one or one-thirty.

At one exactly, I called my editor, Lewis Rosten, to let him know I was at my desk if he wanted to touch and see me.

Moments later, the diminutive Mississippian appeared, unsmiling, in front of my desk.

Lewis reminds me of Truman Capote either having gone straight, or never having gone at all. He was wearing striped suspenders, a polka-dot bow tie, Harry Truman eyeglasses.

"A beard!" he drawled thickly. "That's *exactly* what you didn't need." He slipped away, back in the direction of his own office. "Come," he called.

I went down to his office and he was already on the phone to our executive editor, Moses Reed.

Rosten's office is cluttered with old newspapers and assorted antebellum memorabilia; it looks like the parlor of a Margaret Mitchell devotee. I sat down, noticing a new, or at least uncovered, sign over his desk.

What the Good Lord
lets happen,
I'm not afraid to
print in my paper.
　　　　　　—Mr. Charles A. Davis

That sign, notwithstanding Mr. Davis, was vintage Lewis Rosten.

"Ochs is back," he was saying over the phone. He turned to catch me perusing a 1921 *Citizen.* "Moses wants to know what you've turned up?"

"A lot of things." I smiled.

"A lot of things," he told Reed. "Yeah, don't I know it," he added. I winced.

Lewis hung up the phone and banged out a sentence on his old battered Royal. "The quick brown fox. You and me and Reed. The Honorable Francis Marion Parker. Arnold. Michael Cooder. Up on seven in twenty minutes," he said. "Big strategy session. What have you got? Anything new?"

I took out the photograph of Thomas Berryman. "I have this."

Lewis held the picture about three inches under his nose and eyeglasses. "Hmmm ... Mr. Thomas Berryman, I presume."

I nodded and stayed with my 1921 paper.

"I'd like to get some copies of this. What I'd like to do is run it around to all the hotels later. Look at these, will you."

He handed me a telephone toll call check. Also some kind of credit card check through American Express.

The credit card slip showed that Thomas J. Berryman had charged seven flights on Amex number 041-220-160-1-100AX since January 1.

His flights had been to Port Antonio, Jamaica; Port-au-Prince; Amarillo, Texas; Caneel Bay; and London. None of the flights were to anywhere near Nashville.

"Fuck," I muttered.

The phone check showed one call made to the Walter Scott Hotel in Nashville on June 9th.

"This is pretty interesting. He called here at least."

Rosten didn't comment. He was collecting paperwork for the big meeting.

"From the looks of that credit card thing, the man lives pretty damn well." He finally spoke. "What do people up there think he does?"

"Some people seem to think he works as a lawyer. Not too many people know him."

Rosten put the photograph up to his face again. "I s'pose he could be a lawyer, though?"

"No, Lewis . . . He's a killer."

Rosten rocked back and forth in his own swivel chair, smiling, puffing on his pipe. "Now this," he said like some Old South storyteller, "is what we used to call a barnburner."

"Barnburner's for basketball," I grinned. "You never went to a basketball game in your life."

"No," Rosten smiled wider. "But I heard a lot about them."

He stood up, and we started our walk to the executive editor's office. Calmly puffing his pipe, picking motes and strings off his white shirt, Lewis reminded me to try to be politic.

• • •

Moses Reed is what people of a certain age around Tennessee, men and women, would call "a man's man."

He's tall, always well-dressed, with wavy black hair just hinting at gray. He may have played football somewhere or other—Princeton, I'd heard somewhere—and though under six feet tall, he's considerably broader than I am. He appears to come from money.

His office looks like a wealthy man's dining room. Only some photographs of famous men (Ernest Hemingway kicking a can up a solitary road ... Churchill smoking a cigar in a high-rimmed bathtub ... Bobby Kennedy playing football) spoil the dining room effect.

There is no desk in the office; and no typewriter.

There are antique chairs with embroidered seats. Plus an oblong mahogany table for tea. And a Sheffield tea service.

It's difficult to imagine Reed as a ragamuffin growing up in Birmingham, Alabama—which he was.

Seven of us sat at the highly polished table. A work session. Everyone in crisply starched shirttails except me.

Francis Parker, the conservative *Citizen* publisher—peevish, but a fair man, I'd heard; Reed, transplanted Georgetown journalist, the executive editor; Arnold Beckton, the managing editor; Rosten, metropolitan editor; two other up-and-coming editors; and Ochs Jones, shooting star of the moment.

This was journalism by committee. It's always a disaster. No exceptions.

My heart was in my throat. I kept clearing my throat and trying to catch my breath. The attempts to catch my breath made me yawn.

A stooped black lady was pouring coffee and giving each of us a fresh-sugared cruller. The middle-aged Sunday editor was spouting wit from *Sports Illustrated* stories as though it was essential wisdom.

The mood of the room was jovial right up until the coffee lady left.

Then the jokes stopped abruptly. Each of the others solemnly shook my hand and congratulated me. Reed said a few introductory remarks about the importance of the story I was working on. Then he opened up the floor for questions. They came like a flood.

Was Ben Toy's testimony reliable? Was I sure?

Why hadn't we been able to trace down Harley John Wynn thus far?

Who had hired Berryman?

Where was Berryman right now?

Had anything been done to follow up on the story of the Shepherd brothers out in Washington?

How did the Philadelphia gunman fit in? Did Ben Toy know him?

Exactly what did I think had happened on the day of the shooting? How was young Bert Poole connected?

I answered about eighty-five percent of their questions, but that isn't necessarily a winning percentage in a meeting like that. At least two of the editors were trying to score points by throwing me stumpers.

I began to make excuses for some of the things I'd done. Then quite suddenly Reed was standing over me at the table.

He was smiling like a genial master of ceremonies, turning one of his editors' serious and valid questions into a cute little joke. I felt like a vaudeville comedian about to get the hook. Reed had stopped me in midsentence.

"That's fine," the broad-shouldered man said. His fingers were moving lightly on my arm.

"I think that's just fine, Ochs." He pointed down the table to Lewis Rosten. "We have a few exhibits to show all of you now."

Very suddenly, I understood the purpose of the meeting. It was all a show. All theater for the publisher's benefit.

Lewis dutifully passed around the credit card and phone checks on Berryman; then the photographs of Harley Wynn; finally the picture of Thomas Berryman and a typed report he'd written on the story's progress. His report was just long enough, I noticed, not to be read right away.

Francis Parker was nodding thoughtfully. He asked Rosten a few informal questions and I found myself being talked to by Reed.

"Don't you be hesitant to call me, even at my home," was one of the things he said. "I expect you'll have to go back up North again. Is that all right?"

I said that it was what I had in mind and Reed took my shoulder again. He was emotionally involved, and I couldn't believe how much so.

We both caught the last of what the publisher was saying. Because of the general tone of the meeting, it sounded both important and dramatic.

"Right on through since 1963, every newspaper in this country has been trying to break a story like this one. None of them has . . . I believe, however," he said, "that Moses, Lewis Rosten, and Mr. Ochs are about to do it right here."

Mr. Ochs or Mr. Jones, I remained keyed up for the rest of the day.

I finally got started home around seven that night.

My eyes were tired, watery, blurring up Nashville's streets and traffic. Tex Ritter's Chuckwagon, Ernest Tubb's Records, Luby's Cadillacs flashed out and welcomed me home. I was yawning in a way that could have dislocated my jaw.

Nan tells the story that I put my head down in the middle of dinner and went to sleep beside the roast beef. I remember finishing dessert, so that much of her story is exaggeration.

On the other hand, I don't remember anything much past finishing dinner that night.

I do remember one other phrase of Nan's. "It's like somebody trying to become somebody who other people wish they were," she said.

She didn't say that I was trying to become a newspaper superstar; she just made her statement.

Nashville, July 15

I had slept in my white suit on the living room couch.

A white platter of glistening pork sausage and eggs passed by my eyes as they opened on morning. Canadian geese flew over a lake under the sausage.

My little Cat sat down on the quilt somebody had used to cover me up the night before.

She'd brought sausage, eggs, waffles and strawberries, a Peter Pan glass filled to the brim with bubbly milk.

"Hi, sugar."

"Hi." With that nice look kids get when they're partially off somewhere in their minds.

"Hey," I said. "You awake?"

"I cooked you pancakes and eggs didn't I."

"Oh, yeah," I quickly figured out the sitch. "I'm the one who's not awake."

I took a tricky little bite of waffles and strawberries.

"Mmmff," I drooled. "Tasth jus lith waffleth 'n' strawbearth."

Cat punched me in the side. Misnomer: *love tap*.

She lay in my lap and looked upside down into the new beard. Her little-owl eyeglasses were being held together with a Band-Aid.

"Mom's mad," she said.

"Mmm hmmm. Where's Janie Bug at?"

Not too long after the question was raised, our five-year-old appeared in the hall leading to the kitchen. She had a piece of rye toast stuck in her face.

"Right here," she managed.

"It's beautiful outside," she continued after a bite.

"How do you know that, Buggers?"

"How do I know that, Daddy? I just took Mister Jack for a walk. He went to the bathroom in Mrs. Mills' packajunk again.

"By the way." She pushed her way onto the couch. "The paperboy threw the *Tennessean* at me on Tuesday."

It goes like that at my house. More often than not, I like it very much. In fact, I'm still amazed that I have children.

That's one of the reasons I wound up in Poland County, Kentucky, writing all this down.

Nan came downstairs before nine and I could tell she wasn't that mad. Not at me anyway.

She'd brushed out her long farmgirl's hair, put on the smallest tic of makeup, put on an Indian blouse of hers I like very much.

Nan is a tall, klutzy lady who happens to make as much sense as anybody I've bumped into yet on this planet. We were married when we were both sophomores at the University of Kentucky, and I haven't regretted it yet.

"I had a funny dream, Ochs," she said; she was sitting with Cat and Janie on the couch. "You and James Horn were riding on a raft on a river. Somewhere in the South it looked like. I was there . . . I watched you both through kudzu on the shore. You were talking quietly about something. Something sad and important it looked like. Individual words were carrying on the river, but I couldn't make out the sentences. Then both of you floated out of sight," she said.

After the kids' breakfast, Nan admitted she was glad I was doing the story, though. She'd done volunteer work for Horn once and she'd liked him quite well. Besides that was the fact that Horn's daughter, Keesha, was a best friend of Cat's in school.

The four of us spent all day Saturday at a clambake out in Cumberland, Tennessee.

Lewis Rosten and his graduate school girlfriend were there, and spirits and hopes were high as Mr. Jack Daniels could bring them.

Lewis and I spent part of the day under a shade tree, figuring out how a possible lead story might go. Even that couldn't bring us down though.

Before the sun set Moses Reed showed up in his big, shiny Country Squire. For the first time since I'd come to the *Citizen-Reporter* in 1966, I thought we were a family.

On Sunday morning I took a long, solitary walk over to Nashville's Centennial Park. Once there I tried to draft a story that could work with what I'd gotten from Ben Toy up to then.

It turned out to be a hearsay story. Very exciting, but with the danger of no follow-up.

The lead read:

A NEW YORK MAN SAID TO BE CONNECTED WITH A HIGH-PRICED GUNMAN CLAIMS THAT MAYOR JIMMIE HORN WAS NOT SHOT BY BERT POOLE HERE LAST THURSDAY.

I thought the *Citizen* might run something like that, but I hoped we could open up with a story we wouldn't have to back off of later.

Lewis Rosten stopped by at the house while I was packing up to go back North that night. He seemed as restless about the story as I was. He kept referring to it as "a mystery story."

Rosten told me that the editor-in-chief of the *Nashville Tennessean* had called Reed that afternoon. He'd wanted to know why we were sending reporters around to every hotel and motel in central Tennessee.

"That's all we need," I said. "To get scooped on this."

Rosten didn't want to discuss the possibility. He waved it away like a nauseous man being presented with dessert.

"We checked out every single hotel. Every motel," he said. "We've shown his photograph everywhere a man can sleep in a twenty-five-mile radius."

"Yeah . . . and?"

"Goose egg."

PART II

The End of the Funniest Man in America

West Hampton, July 17

That Monday in West Hampton I could smell northern winters.

The rusty white thermometer on Bowditch's front porch said 67.

I had a feeling that the St. Louis Cardinals were going to get into the World Series; that Ali was going to beat George Foreman. It was all in the air.

It was July 17th and this was to be my last visit with Toy. Our subject was the whereabouts of the southern contact man, Harley John Wynn.

We set up my Sony cassette recorder on a redwood table out in the exercise yard. Its leather traveling case made it look official and important. Historical.

The two of us sat on hardwood deck chairs. Our respective sport shirts off, facing into a lukewarm ball of off-yellow sun.

The sun was just on the verge of overcoming the morning's chill.

Ronald Asher slumped up against a dwarf oak at the center of the yard, growing disenchanted with news reporting I could see. It wasn't exactly as Hunter Thompson had anti-romanticized it in *Rolling Stone*.

A slight breeze turned oak leaves, lifted the blond hair on Toy's forehead, softly bristled my beard.

Ben Toy leaned back and closed his eyes. He was king of the hospital.

After a minute watching five or six contented-looking mental patients sunbathing around the yard, I closed my eyes too.

This was privilege, I was thinking. This was interviewing Elizabeth Taylor over breakfast in a flowery Puerto Vallarta courtyard.

"Tom Berryman never did know it." Toy alternately sucked in the morning air and sniffled. "But on and off for about six months I'd been seeing this wiggy Jewish lady . . . this shrink in New York."

I opened my eyes and saw that Toy was looking at me too. "Why didn't Berryman know?" I asked.

"Because he would have had a shit fit. He wanted me around because I was dependable. He didn't have to worry when I was handling details for him. I was backup.

"So I had to be very careful about this lady. It was all on the sly. All my visits. It was all about me getting depressed. No big shit anyway.

"I went to see her the Wednesday after we'd met Harley Wynn in Massachusetts. I was feeling like a dishrag again. She usually gave me some pills. Valiums. Stelazines.

"This was the day the walls came tumbling down on my head . . . I remember how it was real sunny. Nice out. I wouldn't have believed it was going to turn into such a shit day . . ."

New York City, June 14

Toy's doctor was a Park Avenue psychiatrist, a seventy-year-old woman who preferred being called Reva to Doctor Baumwell.

She saw all her patients at a luxury apartment in a pre-war building on the corner of East 74th Street. She always wore dark dresses and red high-heeled shoes for her appointments.

In his six months with Reva Baumwell, Ben Toy had never once spoken about Thomas Berryman.

For her part, Reva talked of little else except rebuilding Toy's personality. This was "getting as common as face-lifting" she said in an unguarded moment. She also forewarned him that this rebuilding process would probably involve a crisis for him. She was continually asking him if he was about ready for a little crisis, a little pesonality change for the better.

Sometimes, Toy considered the psychiatrist certifiable herself. But she dispensed tranquilizers like vitamin pills, and Ben Toy believed in Valium, in Stelazine and Thorazine. They had a proven track record. They worked for him.

When he left Reva Baumwell's apartment building that day he had a prescription for twenty milligrams of Stelazine in the pocket of his peach nik-nik shirt. Basically, he was feeling pretty good about life.

Then he saw Harley Wynn again.

This time Wynn didn't run away. He was leaning against a silver Mercedes parked in front of the building's awning. The smug look on his face brought to mind F.B.I. agents harassing hippie dope dealers.

The two of them met under the building's long shadow.

"I saw you on East End Avenue too," Wynn said in a drawl that seemed to be thickening. "You see, I've been thinking about last week. I decided you were a little too abrupt with me . . . So I've been following you around. I've seen Berryman."

Ben Toy's impulse was to sucker-punch Wynn right there. To smash his head across the car hood.

"I want to talk to him," the southern man continued. "Face to face . . . we have things to discuss about Jimmie Horn."

Toy lighted up a cigarette, "Where did you see Berryman?" he asked.

"Outside of Eighty Central Park South," Harley Wynn said. "He was with this tall girl. Foxy lady. They caught a cab."

"All right," Toy said.

Together, they started walking toward 72nd Street. Toy stopped at a corner phone booth on 72nd and called Berryman.

Berryman listened to the whole story before he said a word.

"That's his fuck-up," was what Toy remembered him saying first. "I'd have to say it's your fuck-up too," he went on. "I think you know the alternatives. I hope you do anyway."

Berryman hung up on him, but Toy held the receiver to his ear an extra minute or two. His head was reeling.

Then Toy swung open the phone booth door and smiled at the young southerner for the first time. What he said was, "Everything's cool. Berryman said it was my fuck-up . . . He wants to talk to you this afternoon."

•   •   •

A little after three o'clock that afternoon, Ben Toy sat beside the slightly younger Wynn in the crackling red leather seat of an Olds 98.

Toy was thinking that his mind was going to snap. Crack like somebody's backbone.

The shiny black sedan was parked in bright sun in a Flushing junkyard near La Guardia Airport. It was all flat, baking weeds over to dismal, sagging high-risers a mile or so away.

Harley Wynn kept saying that Berryman was late. Five minutes late. Ten minutes late. Fifteen minutes late.

A white Chevy came barrel-assing down the dirt road leading into the junkyard. It was doing seventy or eighty, then it skidded and u-turned. Kids. Joy-riders.

"Y'see Tom Berryman is real concerned with his own safety," Ben Toy explained to Wynn. "He's a real brain. Takes zip chances. He's obsessed sometimes. But he'll be here. Don't worry. Stop worrying."

Wynn had his arm across the back of the leather seat and he was looking off at the apartment buildings. His head was at a good angle for a portrait. He was showing his nice white teeth just right.

"I'm sure Berryman doesn't take chances," he said.

The two men were sitting around, talking like that, and then Ben Toy very suddenly reached out of his jacket, and shot Harley Wynn in the side of the forehead.

The action was completed totally on impulse. Toy kept saying *now, now, now, now,* and when it felt real, when he believed it somewhere in his body, a small black .38 flashed out, the trigger snapped back. The sound was deafening, a sound Toy would never forget. Pink flesh and blood splatted onto the vinyl roof and the windshield. Wynn's head went out the open window and hung there.

Toy left the southerner spreadeagled across a pink flowered box spring in the junkyard. His blond hair wasn't even mussed.

Before driving away, Toy had the presence of mind to fire a second shot into the back of Wynn's head. That second shot distorted the handsome face considerably.

Because of that second, meaningless bullet, the evening papers in New York reported the killing as gangland style. No identification was found on Wynn. No one claimed the body until November. By that time, it was hopelessly lost in Potter's Field. New York simply sent a large skeleton down to Tennessee.

Directly after the shooting, Ben Toy called Berryman to tell him it was done.

Then Toy spent four days in Mill House Sanitarium in upstate New York. He barely spoke to anyone at the private hospital, especially the doctors. He sat around a sunny parlor overlooking the Hudson River, and whatever he was feeling got worse.

Toy thought he was the only person at the hospital who wasn't drying out. Who wasn't getting B_{12} shots. He was also the only one hallucinating. One afternoon he heard a black woman's voice that announced it was James Horn's mother. One night in his room he heard his father's voice and saw flashes of light outside his window.

Very confused in his mind, he walked off to get a drink one afternoon. He strolled down a country road with farms and seminaries all around. He eventually called Reva Baumwell from a tavern under rocky mountains over the Hudson.

"I told Tom I wouldn't be able to kill anybody," he said. "I was right. I was right this time. That fuck thinks anybody can do it. Shit, everybody isn't built that way. Jesus Christ, I'm hearing voices, Reva." He almost started crying over the phone. He was losing control and it was horrible.

"One message at a time," Doctor Baumwell said. "What's *kill?* Hurt someone, you mean? Hurt who, Benjamin? Hurt yourself? Hurt me?"

• • •

Thomas Berryman watched teenagers crowding the steps of Carnegie Hall. A silvery sign with attached glossy photos announced that Blue Oyster Cult was appearing that evening.

Berryman was in a pay phone directly across the street from the concert hall on 57th Street. He was calling a man in the Belle Meade section of Nashville, Tennessee.

A gruff southern man's voice finally came on the other end of the line.

Berryman spoke in a slow, deliberate monotone. He gave out his name. He said he was calling in reference to a man named Harley Wynn.

"What about him?" The southern man seemed to be an authoritarian.

"He's dead. I just had to have him shot," Berryman continued the monotone.

The southern man's voice cracked. "You had him what?"

A city bus applied loud air brakes a few feet from the glass booth window. Berryman found himself looking at a naked blond man promoting *Viva* magazine on the side of the bus. "Hello, hello?" he could hear in the receiver.

The bus started up with a sick, heavy grumble.

"You knew my rules," Berryman began to talk again. "I don't know what Wynn saw around here. He was supposed to pay us some money, then go back to Tennessee."

"Well, I don't know about that part," the southerner said. "He told me he had other business keeping him in New York. I had no intention of interfering with you."

"I don't believe you," Berryman said flatly. He'd decided to take the offensive.

"Goddamnit, I didn't," the other man exploded. "Listen you . . ." he started to say.

Berryman raised his voice over the man's next few words. "I've already begun on your business. I have your money," he said, "the first half anyway. I've had to spend some of it. Do you want me to continue?"

The southerner spoke without hesitation. "Of course continue. Go on with it. Wynn is a very small part of this thing."

"I'm planning to be in Nashville the first week, the last week in June," Berryman said. "You should have the remaining money. You won't hear from me until then."

The southerner added a few conditions of his own. Then the phone call was over.

Berryman took a long, deep breath. He'd momentarily lost control of the situation, but now he had it back.

He left the booth running a white comb back through his curly black hair.

• • •

I don't know at what point, but at a definite point, within the span of say five minutes, Ben Toy began to talk indiscriminately about anything that came into his head.

He talked about mathematics, about God—I think, about his parents in Texas, my nineteen-fiftyish oxblood loafers, lobotomies, Martin Luther King . . . all kinds of ridiculous, moronic things that didn't coordinate.

It was scary, because I'd started to believe there was nothing really wrong with Toy.

"My mother used to dance in Reno, Nevada," he spoke very seriously to me. "That's why nobody in Potter County wanted to take her out for a goddamn celery soda."

I slowly stood up, no shirt on or anything, and I called Asher.

He came, and then three more aides came running. They walked Toy back onto the hall, and he went quietly, meekly. I finally turned off the Sony, which had been silently going about its business.

Ronald Asher was closing the heavy quiet room door when I arrived on the hall. The other three aides and a nurse who was just a young girl were standing around with him.

"He broke off a fucking needle in his ass," Asher said.

I gave him an uncomprehending look and peeked in through the observation window.

"Annie gave him the needle, and then he just flip-flopped over on it."

"It came out," the young nurse said.

"Jesus," I said. "I don't believe the way he just . . . went off. Poof."

"Believe it," the nurse smiled.

"I don't know where Ben's head is," Asher said: "Shulman thinks he knows."

"Too much Psilocybin," a tall aide in a Levi's shirt said.

"A lot of patients just let their minds run loose when they're in here," Asher said. "Some of them are crazy because it feels better is my theory. Fuck my theories though."

Looking back through the observation window, I watched as Toy suddenly jumped up in the air. He floated on his back, then drop-kicked the screen window with his bare feet. He repeated this stunt several times, his back *whopping* the narrow mattress on each fall.

"It won't hurt him," Asher said without looking in. "I think it calms him down. Like the way little kids rock in their beds."

The young nurse looked at me and shrugged.

"My daughter does that," I said. "Rocks in her bed, I mean . . ."

The nurse asked me how old she was. We went back to the glass-encased station and joked our way back toward normalcy. The girl had never had a needle broken off on her before.

· · ·

I'd walked to the hospital, and I walked back, cutting a diagonal across the grounds, then going into some woods.

I climbed a tall, forbidding fence at the end of the woods. Darted and stalked across the Long Island Expressway. Made private discoveries in the face of speeding headlights.

Back at the motel, I drew myself a steamy, hot bath. I climbed in and things slowly began to come back into perspective.

I remembered another mad scene I'd witnessed. It was in a snooker hall and gin mill in Frankfurt, Kentucky. (At that time, in '62 I think, I was carrying a small pistol myself, so I was no great judge of madness.)

What happened was this.

A scarecrow-looking farmboy in the bar had decided he was going to sneak a dance with this other boy's girl. They started dancing to this slow Elvis Presley song that was popular back then, "One Night" I think it was, and when the other boy saw what was happening, he walked up to the dancing couple, spit in the scarecrow's face, and then stabbed him in the crotch area. Just that quick.

Everybody in the bar immediately crowded around the crumpled clothes and body on the dance floor, and with hot eyes and crying, and low whispers, they kept repeating around the circle that *Old Bean* had been *stoh-bbed*.

If you had taken that word's meaning from its tone, you'd have guessed that the pleasures of dance and whiskey had been too much for Bean, and that he'd passed out.

Pistol on and all, I'd nearly thrown up on the spot.

• • •

The news about the Harley Wynn photograph came while I was up to my neck in hot bathwater and suds. I was reading single pages out of Jeb Magruder's book on his life & Watergate, then putting it to rest on the lip of the tub. I found it infuriating that he'd had the cunning to churn out the book so quickly.

The news came when I was melancholy, sentimental as country music, missing Nan and Cat and Janie Bug like close friends moved out of town.

It couldn't have come at a better time if I'd been in charge of planning my own life.

The phone rang in the bedroom and I just let it ring. I thought it was Asher or that nurse checking on me.

It kept right on ringing, a little red light buzzing with it.

"Terrell," I heard when I finally picked it up. "That shitheel, cocksucker Terrell."

The distant voice on the phone was Lewis Rosten's. It wasn't Rosten's normal speaking voice, though. Rosten was rarely if ever vulgar.

I tried to knock a cigarette out of a pack and four or five tumbled out.

"What about Terrell?"

"Ochs, *Harley Wynn is Terrell's man*. He's his lawyer. He's from Houston is the reason nobody knew him."

Rosten had started to shout. He was very happy. I was nervously lighting up one of the cigarettes.

"You did it this time, you smart bastard," I heard. "Reed says he could and will kiss your ass on television. Your sweet ass."

Somebody else was on the line. Happy rebel yells was who it was.

I was holding the receiver away from my ear, starting to giggle like the big fucking village idiot.

More people came on the line with congratulations.

"How did it break?" I kept asking each new voice. "How did it break?"

"Complicated." I eventually got Lewis back. "Some friend of Reed's is from Houston. Who cares!"

I was just beginning to figure out the ramifications and I couldn't believe it. It seemed so perfectly right and logical. *Johnboy Terrell*.

"Let me have some damn enthusiasm," quiet little Rosten yelled over the phone.

I obliged him. I went partially, happily berserk at Hojo's in West Hampton, Long Island.

I gave out some rebel hoots and howls that had people knocking at me through the motel walls. I crowhopped around the rug on my big bare feet. I kicked the walls like somebody on their way home from *Singin' in the Rain*.

Before I go any farther, though, I should tell you that during the years 1958 to 1962 Terrell was governor of the state; that from about 1958 on, Terrell had just about run Tennessee; and that some people, myself included, thought that he had run it very, very badly.

What's more, Terrell certainly had a major grudge to settle with Jimmie Horn.

That night, my batteries all recharged, I wrote up a long, inspired list of follow-up calls and visits I still had to make in the North. For the very first time, I felt totally comfortable with the story.

I prepared for a trip out to Berryman's summer house in a place called Hampton Bays. It was there that I was to make my one big mistake in judgment while recording this story.

PART III

The Girl Who Loved Thomas Berryman

Hampton Bays, July 20

Thomas Berryman's house at Hampton Bays was a sprawling, storm-gray sea captain's house with a long canopied porch and five hundred feet of private beach-front. There were separate garages all over the place. The garages were literally everywhere you looked.

Inside the ten-bedroom house I found an unexpected surprise: Berryman's girlfriend, a strange, beautiful lady named Oona Quinn.

A modern woman I guess you could call her, Oona Quinn was growing up in the manner of young men: she was groping, grappling, scratching for what she considered her rightful place in the world. That's why Thomas Berryman liked her, I imagine.

Oona is tall and thin. (5'9", big bones, 130 pounds.) She has flowing black hair that can come below her waist, but she generally keeps it up in a large bun. She has the classic, stately look of New England, and the best of it. She'll smoke brown cigarettes, however, letting them hang out of the side of her mouth.

Unlike Ben Toy, Oona was the kind of person I'd known in my own life. She'd been a clerk in a boutique the spring and winter before she met Berryman. But she was bright with common sense. She was the one, for example, who finally gave me a reasonable explanation why *beautiful people* are forever hugging. She said it was their way of breaking sexual tensions. I liked that idea.

Oona Quinn said she was twenty, and that was a startling, but possible, fact.

I first saw her through a screen door, a black, dirty screen in the kitchen. I had my eyes and nose up against it and the shadowy outline of her hair was wild and bushy. A beautiful witch, I thought. I called inside.

During our first moments in the doorway—as I explained how I'd come to the house via Ben Toy—I scratched my nose, took a deep breath, scratched my chin, my ear, blinked several times, brushed the shoulder of my jacket, and lit a cigarette.

"Haven't you ever seen a woman before?" she asked. I laughed (embarrassing memory) and said, "Uh course."

At the outset, Oona was reluctant to talk about anything—even the kind of day it was, or wasn't, or ought to be. This didn't surprise me, of course.

We walked down to the water on a gray picket fence that was laid flat instead of standing up. She carried a little kitchen radio that was playing cabaret songs, and it was almost as if I wasn't there.

After we'd tramped a good distance from the house she asked me some questions. "What . . . exactly what did Ben Toy tell you?" she said.

I didn't see a good reason to hold anything back, so I told her most of what I knew. She listened to it all, and then she simply laughed.

"He's crazy, you know. Tuned out."

"He said you know what happened in Nashville," I told her.

"He said?" she stopped walking and turned to me. "Or are you figuring things out by yourself, Mr. Jones?"

She drifted away without an answer. Over closer to the water so it ran up over her feet. Her toes were long and bony with spots of red polish on the nails. And she *was* outrageously attractive.

When we finally reached a point out of sight of the house she plopped down in the sand. "Lili Marlene" came on her radio and she turned it up full.

"I feel very . . . like wind and things can pass right through me. It's very weird talking to you right now. Unreal," she said with a big sigh.

I asked her if Berryman was around somewhere and she gave no answer.

And then for some reason (I wasn't able to understand it until I'd gathered more information) Oona Quinn began to tell me little things about herself. She spoke cautiously at first. In a cynical, irreverent sort of way. But after a while I started to get the feeling that I was hearing a nervous, maybe even a contrite confession. I also got the feeling that the girl was scared and confused.

She and I spent nearly three days together in Thomas Berryman's house, and she spoke more and more freely (I thought) about what had happened between herself and Berryman.

One time she called him "the master of good vibes." She said that he had a ten-inch prick, if that question was circulating around my mind. And she also said that I tended to be gloomy.

All in all it was a crazy environment for me. For one thing, I'd never spent a lot of time with beautiful women before; for another, the only other time I'd been at the seashore was in Biloxi, Mississippi. I also had trouble sleeping. At night, it got cold as Tennessee winter out there.

During our second day go-round, Oona told me that Bert Poole hadn't shot Jimmie Horn.

"Ben Toy told me the same thing," I said.

"He doesn't know." She disputed that. "He thinks Tom's going to come take him back to Texas in the Mercedes."

* * *

The back porch ran along the entire length of the house, and that was where we usually talked. We would sit on wicker porch furniture, facing out at the ocean. Thinking about it now, I can remember her bony, wool-socked toes wiggling in and out of leather clogs. It was her nervous tic, she said.

More often than not, a khaki-uniformed gardener would be working on the lawns as we taped.

A rangy, suspicious Jamaican, he thought I was getting into Oona's pants behind Berryman's back. He was fiercely loyal to Thomas Berryman, and said it was none of my damn business how come, mon.

One afternoon I noticed Oona handing the man several twenty-dollar bills. It gave me the uncomfortable feeling that Berryman was somewhere close by, supervising, maybe watching us from the mountainous dunes all around his house.

For her part, Oona Quinn would shrink up all vulnerable and wallflower-like whenever we talked. She'd sit on her long legs, hugging herself. She'd rock, and the wicker chair and porch would creak in unison.

She'd be very much in control, even haughty, until I pulled the tape recorder from its leather case. But something about the tape recorder got to her. Something about having her words recorded put a big, hard lump in her throat.

She was a lively storyteller though; she had a natural sense for ironic detail. I thought, in fact, that she was feeling ironic about herself, and I hoped to use that to get closer to Thomas Berryman.

Hampton Bays, June 18

Under a fat red sun, Thomas Berryman straddled the roof of his sea captain's house and watched down where white-caps were breaking all over a rough, stony Atlantic Ocean. The high air was clean, thick with salt, blue to look at. It was late June now.

Working at about fifty percent consciousness, Berryman's mind kept drifting back to sugary Sunday school scenes from Texas. He wondered what was becoming of himself.

After a while, his eyes focused on a small piece of tar patchwork he'd completed, and he thought it was good work to patch your own roof. His gardener had refused to do the high roofing job, and now Berryman was pleased.

He looked over at sand dunes—rising fifty or sixty feet on the other side of the highway—and his eyes followed a white Mustang tooling along the pigeon-gray road at their base. The Mustang scampered away between the sand hills like a cartoon car. At one time, Berryman remembered, he'd threatened his father with bodily harm over the issue of a Ford Mustang.

He lit a rare cigarette and let himself float in warm, afternoon sensations. He could see Oona walking down on

the beach in a white string suit. Very chic-chic. Now and
again his mind drifted to the subject of Jimmie Horn.

He shimmied over to the dark stone (cool) chimney,
and began to install a new screen over its big mouth.

Because the old penny loafers he was wearing slipped
on the roof slates, he had to ride the apex horseback style.
The danger of possibly slipping off the three-story roof—
missing the sun porch—hitting patio furniture that looked
the size of pocket change—was part of the job and part
of its pleasure.

He placed his face inside the musky hole and in the
light of a match saw that the chimney screen was clogged
closed with soot. With sooty sand. With sooty seagull
feathers and a child's deflated balloon.

The white Ford sports car passed down on the road
again. He flicked his cigarette butt at it, then yanked up
the chimney debris with both hands on the inky screen.

He and Oona ate a good dinner of white spaghetti and
red wine. He drew on a stogie joint and passed it to her
across their dinner table on the front lawn. They were both
dressed rather hautily, in white, and together looked like
a page out of a fashion magazine.

On closer examination, he was wearing red, white, and
blue track shoes. Oona was wearing no makeup. She had
promised to chase his blues away that night.

"Oh," she said before beginning her exorcism, "Ben
Toy called." Her lips were slightly blistered from sunbathing. She drew daintily on the fat joint.

Tom Berryman held smoke in as he spoke. "While I was on the roof?"

"Didn't believe me when I told him . . . that you were on the roof. Sounded weird."

Berryman continued to hold the smoke in.

"All he said was, something about, he read about the Horns. What good people the Horns are. Who are the Horns?"

Berryman blew out smoke and talked to himself. ". . . Ben's flipping out on me."

"Yeah?"

"Yeah."

Oona passed the cigarette and cocked her head like a pretty bird. "So who are the Horns?"

"They're nobody," Berryman said. He took up the joint. His eyes twinkled with dope dust. "Really they're twins," he smiled. "We used to go out with them in Amarillo. Patsy and Darlene, High Plains High," He started to laugh. "Darlene had a pretty little red mustache. Nice personality, too." He laughed some more. "Great little talker, that girl."

Oona got the giggles, and then they both forgot about Ben Toy. He forgot his blues. They indulged in a freak rift that would have put good southern writers to shame. Berryman told a story in which a family's grandmother dies on a long car trip, and the father puts her in the trunk so that the kids won't know, and the car gets stolen at Hojo's with grandma in the trunk. He said it was true.

• • •

Hours later, Oona Quinn sat stoned, looking at his face. Berryman held both her breasts in his hands, feeling them through her blouse, testing their weight.

A burning oak log gave the bedroom a smell like backwoods. The curtains on the open windows ballooned in the night breeze.

She stared at cool, splintering blue eyes.

A thick bushy mustache that wasn't well groomed.

A flickering, pearly smile that caused her to smile back.

She imagined Thomas Berryman as one of Clark Gable's sons. And she imagined, or remembered, a strange man who kept caged crickets to simulate the backwoods in his bedroom.

"Bugfucker," Berryman commented when she told him. She sucked and ate crickets like the French candies with hard shells and gooey centers. She thought there was nothing she wouldn't like to try.

"Ever been married?" he asked her in response to that.

"No. You?"

"I guess," Berryman smiled up with his eyes closed. "For about seventeen days in high school. It wasn't religious or legal bound. Lived in a treehouse if I remember right. Say," he went on, "you said that Benboy called before? You said that, right? You said that?"

The bedroom where he and Oona Quinn were lying was the plainest space in the house. It was a wide place with a low, wood-beamed ceiling, a small fieldstone fireplace, and white rows of library shelves stacked with bound-up *National Geographic*s and *American Scholar*s (from a past owner).

The one small window (it is clouded with salt) looked out on the ocean, while a big bay window faced up the long narrow highway. Berryman said that the house had been spun assbackward in a hurricane and/or it had been built by assholes. Take your pick.

Oona slipped an expensive peasant's blouse up over her hair, and her tiny breasts popped out of the folds one at a time. They were white and startling.

"Do you like my boobs tanned or white?" the twenty-year-old in her asked. She was both self-conscious and serious.

Thomas Berryman pinched one nipple and held it up near his chin. He examined it like a grocer with an apple by its stem. "Yes," he said. "Very, very much."

He pulled his own shirt over his head. He was lobster pink from the roofing job. "How do you like my little tit-ties?"

She wrinkled her nose. "You'll look like a black man in a week or so. Except your nose is so waspy."

"I have to kill a blackman."

She laughed. "That gardener. Good, he's a snot."

Berryman knelt in the middle of the bed and kissed her, without touching his pink chest against her.

He told her that ladies in Texas never cursed, and that they always kept scented handkerchiefs in their bosoms, and that they talcumed their rear ends.

Outside the bay window, far across the highway in the sand dunes, Ben Toy sat in darkness on the hood of the white Mustang. He studied the glowing second floor window. In his mind, he was there to protect Tom-Tom and the Irish girl. In return, they had to protect him.

A few times out on the dunes Toy heard a black woman's voice announcing it was James Horn's mother. One time he heard his father. Ben Toy thought he was having a nervous breakdown, and he was right.

Oona and Thomas Berryman continued to smoke the night away, and at a time when neither of them could do much more than nod their overblown heads, he started to ramble about a southern blackman he had been paid to kill.

As he described his plans for the unfortunate man, Oona Quinn threw up on the bed and then conveniently passed out.

Hampton Bays, June 19

In the morning, he was wearing a gray PROPERTY OF NEW YORK KNICKS sweatshirt and looking innocent as a new M.D.

He was ministering to the sick, too. Fluffing feather pillows. Opening old singed shades to bright ocean sunlight.

He carried Oona a pewter pot of coffee and honey cakes

in a different bedroom from the one she'd thrown up in. The two of them didn't have much to say, and only slowly did she realize he'd moved her, and changed her clothes sometime between night and morning. Put her in black tights.

"If you don't want to stay," he said, "you ought to go pretty soon. I had to find out, you know. You don't have to be afraid to leave." He continued to break bags of natural sugar into her coffee. "I've never harmed any friend. Not even anyone I liked. Don't be afraid."

She sipped the steamy coffee and watched him over the cup's rim. Her eyes were slow and sad. Berryman had already figured that if she'd wanted to go, she would have tried to sneak away earlier.

"Coffee all right?"

He frowned at the dumbness of his question.

Oona refused to pout, however, "S'all right," she said. She was drinking it.

"Scumbag," she added after another sip.

Berryman felt obliged to offer her some explanation. "It just gives me too much freedom to stop now," he offered first. "I don't even think I want to.

"I remember when I was ... some teenage year. Eighteen. Seventeen, nineteen . . . I drew up this philosophy. Ben and I did . . . I suppose it was more me than Ben . . .

"It was more complicated, but it really boiled down to—fuck it all. Somebody named me the pleasure king. At least I made a choice," he said.

"Let me put it another way. Take an average person. Approach him with an offer to do what I do. Bad stuff, right? All kinds of immoral. Imagine it, though.

"Say this man is offered fifty to kill a total stranger. Say he has the know-how to do it. That's important for it to be a fair question.

"What do you think would happen? In most cases?"

Oona's chin hadn't moved from the coffee cup. "I don't know," she said.

"That's no answer, babe.

"OK, that's what you think. No, then. He'd call the police, OK?"

Berryman could see she was looking for some killer line. Some way to flush his toilet but good. He wouldn't let her. "So you mean if I put fifty thousand dollars on this bed," he asked her. "Better yet, if I'd left it at that little shop where you worked. Real money. Tens, twenties, fifties. And I'd told you—just to take a weak example— 'get rid of the manager of the Hyannis A&P'? No action, huh? . . ."

She said *scheis.*

"What did you say?"

"Nothing."

"You said something. Say it."

"Nothing. It doesn't matter. *Scheis* means shit in Russian."

"Uh. I don't think so."

Oona Quinn didn't say any more, but she didn't go anywhere, either.

Revere, Massachusetts, July 22

Oona Quinn had grown up in one of a thousand similar claptrap houses in the amusement park town of Revere, Massachusetts. A pop singer named Freddie Cannon had grown up in Revere, too. Then he'd written a hit song about Palisades Park. It was that kind of uninspiring town.

The Quinn house had been bright white, then neutral green, then pale yellow, matching her parents' diminishing regard for their 1955 purchase.

In some ways the house even resembled her father. The grass was cut short, but not trimmed. The Weatherbeater paint job looked passable from the street, but was peeling, scabbing, up close. The front porch was starting to sag; and the screen in the door was torn.

I went out of my way to stop at the Quinns' on my way back from Provincetown that third week in July. I wanted to know what kind of a girl would take up with a young man like Thomas Berryman.

When I first met him, Oona's father was as suspicious and closemouthed as she had been. He made me give him my wallet and we both stood out on the front lawn while he read all the press cards and matched signatures.

"My newspaper is willing to pay you for an interview," I mentioned at one point.

He nodded, but didn't indicate *yes* or *no*. "What do you know about Oona?" he asked me.

"I've met her and talked to her. She told me about you and her mother. She's in some trouble."

"Yeah, I figured that," the man said. He gestured toward the house and I walked behind him to the front steps.

I sat out on the sagging porch with Frankie Quinn for nearly two hours that afternoon. He was a forty-three-year-old man with graying muttonchop sideburns, a flattened pug nose, a considerable two-pillow pouch.

He didn't look like he could possibly be Oona's father.

He worked as a four-to-one A.M. bartender at the Mayflower in South Boston, he told me. But he handled none of the action there: no gambling, no drugs, no prostitutes. He brought home an honest one-sixty-one a week.

He said he'd remained a devout Roman Catholic until the 1960s when the English mass had come in. He'd felt personally betrayed by that, and by the *goom-bi-ya* folk singing.

His personal cross to bear, his family's cross, was his extraordinary thirst for stout. He had what he called a "case a day habit."

His wife, Margaret, and Oona were the two best things that had ever happened to him. He made no bones about it. He wanted to know everything I knew about her, and he wanted to talk about her himself.

So far, so good, I thought. I switched on the Sony.

"I could have been stricter with Oona," Frankie Quinn admitted between sips of Guinness and plunges into a box of Ritz crackers. "She got her own way a little more than most. Because she was so pretty, you know. We may have been too good to her. I don't know if we were or not."

"She's a good kid, a wonderful one. Until she stops hearing how pretty she is. Then she kinda falls apart. Then everything's a downer for her. She never learned to cope if you know what I mean. Maybe she doesn't have to, though. Some people never seem to have to."

"I don't remember that she had many girlfriends growing up. Too many boyfriends. I used to come home Saturday night it looked like a bachelor's party here. All these gazuzus from Cathedral High School. Just waiting for her to tell them to go get her a pistachio ice cream down the store . . ."

"She talks a lot about you," I told Frankie Quinn.

Quinn laughed. His voice went way up into the tenor range.

"We got along ok, me and her. Used to go on these long, long walks down the beach. People staring at me like I'm some Irish Mafioso with his young bird.

"It's Margaret she's got problems with these days. Margaret never got over she doesn't go to church anymore. What the hell, now Margaret doesn't go herself."

Quinn stopped talking and looked hard at me for a moment. He had watery eyes that were always shiny.

"You're Thomas Berryman, aren't you?" he said quite seriously.

I was too startled to answer for a second. I thought he'd gotten tipsy. Then I told him that I wasn't Berryman and went looking for more identification in my wallet.

"No, no." He grabbed my arm and held it out of my pocket. "I knew you weren't. Just had to make sure of it. I got nervous, I guess."

He went on to tell me that Oona had mentioned Berryman to him during several phone calls over the past few months.

Then he brought up Jimmie Horn.

He said Oona had dropped the name during a phone call on July 3rd. Then on the 4th of July he'd read that Jimmie Horn had been murdered down South.

Quinn clarified further. He said that Oona had called him from Tennessee on July 2nd, 3rd, and 4th. He said that she was almost hysterical when she called on the 4th. He wanted me to tell him why, and I told him what I could.

Margaret Quinn came home just after five. Frankie and I were still out on the porch.

Margaret was a slender, dark-haired woman who reminded me of her daughter. I agreed with Frank Quinn's estimate that he was a lucky man.

I also got the feeling that neither one of them had any idea what their daughter had become. In their eyes she was still a high school girl, thought high school girl thoughts, wore plaid jumpers and blue blazers.

I liked the Quinns, but I also felt sorry for them. What was about to happen to them, especially if my story broke nationally, frightened me. Frank and Margaret Quinn were going to be totally unprepared to deal with it.

In general, I just wasn't meeting the kind of bad people I'd expected to be connected with an assassination.

In the meantime, though, I had the problem that Oona Quinn wasn't telling me everything I needed to know. At least maybe she wasn't. And maybe she was lying to me altogether.

I didn't like it at all, but then *it* wasn't asking to be liked.

• • •

I drove back from Massachusetts to New York in a gray-blue rainstorm. It was Saturday night, nearly 6:30 when I began the trip.

The storm came on strong as I was winding away from the Revere amusement park area. The families-with-young-children crowd was just arriving on the opposite side of the street.

The first raindrops were half-dollar-sized, and I had to close up all the car windows in spite of the heat.

The downpour didn't let up once until I was getting off the New London ferry back on Long Island. I began to feel like that L'il Abner character with the personal raincloud that follows him everywhere he goes.

Every light in Berryman's house was burning. Floodlights on top of the garages showed up large patches of white dune grass.

I eased up the driveway, crunching gravel, fantasizing either a party or a suicide.

Oona was sitting all by herself in the front room. She was wrapped up in a red star quilt on the couch, bare feet and head showing, watching the TV.

"Ochs?" she looked at the dark screen door and called. "Is that Ochs?"

I stood on the porch, wondering who else it could be. Then I started to rap on the wood frame around the door. "Anybody home?" I called out. I was acting like I was fresh back from a ten-duck shoot. I was psyched up to talk with her about Tennessee.

She wasn't in the mood for that, though.

"We can talk tomorrow," she said. "Tomorrow's soon enough. You've had enough for tonight, little man."

I sat down in a musty easy chair. "Little man?" I laughed.

She sat across the width of the room wrapped up in her ball of red quilt. She was looking at me kind of funny. Boy-girl funny, I thought.

All scrunched up on the couch, she seemed to be freezing cold. She looked like she wanted someone to cuddle.

Both of us sat there not saying anything. *Easy Rider* was playing on TV, but it was already past the Jack Nicholson part. I was thinking that Oona reminded me of those high-paid and basically overwhelming photographic models . . . only this was the way they were behind the scenes: high-strung, and strung-out.

She watched me with a troubled look on her face. Then she smiled. "I'm going up now," she said.

She made cocoa in the kitchen. Then she slipped up the creaky stairs with a pewter cup sticking out of her quilt like a candle. "Ochs," she called from the top of the stairs, "Tom Berryman isn't going to show up here."

I sat downstairs trying to figure out what she had meant by that. Finally, after another ten minutes or so, I went upstairs to the room I was using.

I sprawled flat-out on a six-foot-long spring bed. My feet were sticking out the iron rungs.

I lay there in my white shirt and boxer shorts, smoking, watching the man in the moon, going a little crazy inside.

It's not my favorite way to relax after a long day, but it's a way.

I tried thinking about some of the things I had to ask her the next day. I couldn't organize those thoughts, though.

I reached back and pulled the chain lamp over my bed.

I took off my shirt and brought a crinkly sheet up around my chin. Itchy new beard. Sandy sheets. Man in the moon looking puffy—like he'd been in a fistfight.

I heard bare feet padding out in the hall.

The bathroom door opened. Sound of the chain lamp in there. Bottles, Charlie and Pot Pourri, tinkling.

She ran herself a tub, and didn't come out again until after I was asleep.

• • •

In the morning it was business as usual. The gardener out in the yard. Toes wiggling in wool socks. Her nervousness before the microphone. My nervousness with her.

Oona said she would tell me anything I wanted to know. She also said that she got a kick out of my 1930s Bible Belt morality. She wasn't being mean, just truthful.

New York City, June 21

Lying around outside Berryman's largest garage, just collecting seagull shit and other natural indignities, there is a black Porsche Targa, a Cadillac, and a mint-condition tan Mercedes 450SE convertible.

Early one morning in the last week of June, Berryman drove Oona into midtown Manhattan in the convertible. The air was thick, gauzy, which was good for hiding housing tracts and cigarette billboards.

The two of them jabbered and kidded for the entire two-hour commute. Hollering over wind and WABC, she told him that she'd become aware she was straightening her hair before mirrors some twenty or twenty-five times a day. But she told the story as a very funny joke.

He finally dropped her off to shop on Fifth Avenue. Watched her floppy yellow skimmer go through the waves of sleepy office workers like an umbrella. Disappear into Lord & Taylor.

Then Berryman used the sluggish blocking of a growling city bus to inch his way up to Central Park South, and (he was hoping) Ben Toy.

Ben Toy wasn't at the Central Park apartment, so Berryman tried to call him at his own apartment. He tried to call him at the Flower & Toy, and at the apartments of lady friends.

He lighted a cigarillo and sat at his work desk, wondering what had happened to Toy. He couldn't remember passing a month without seeing the funniest man in America.

After thinking about Toy for a while, getting as depressed as he allowed himself to get, he went to his wall safe. He look out fifteen fifty-dollar bills and he copied an address from a small red pad kept in with the cash. The address was 88 East End Avenue. Berryman was back in business. The business was Jimmie Horn.

Doubleparked on East 87th Street, he sat on the trunk of the Mercedes, thinking.

Trying not to be distracted by the New York carnival, he *was*, nonetheless. By a businessman riding an expensive bicycle, with a gas mask over his face. His system of empty pipes carried the sign: NON-POLLUTING VEHICLE.

The gas mask struck Berryman's fancy. Once he'd passed Joe Namath and his girlfriend on that same corner. Not a very pretty girl, she'd said, "You don't have to hold my hand" to Namath. So much for fame and football.

Berryman walked past buildings numbered 92, 94, 100—toward 86th Street. He paused at a city litter basket advertising a midwestern beer. He rummaged through the trash. But there was nothing he could use to implement his plan.

At a flashy boutique on 84th, however, he was given a fancy, plastic carryball bag. It was perfect. It would become a mask.

The glass front door of 88 East End was spray-painted Kool Whip 111. This was luxury, New York style. Smoking a long rope cigarillo, Thomas Berryman walked inside. He was trying to look well-to-do and important, and he looked it.

A heavy Puerto Rican security guard announced him from the lobby. The guard was stationed in front of a system of security monitors showing scenes like the garbage pails out back. The man was smoking a fat cigar, looking as official as a Banana Republic general. "A Mister Ben Toy, jes sir?" he said into a small microphone.

A clipped British voice bounced back from upstairs. "Mr. Toy, please come right up."

"Ju can go up now," the doorman said with undaunted authority.

As the elevator cruised efficiently to the thirtieth floor, Berryman carefully poked and dug holes in the plastic bag.

The thirtieth-floor hallway was carpeted, empty, luxuriously quiet. As Berryman looked for the apartment marked M. Romains, he slipped on the plastic bag. He pulled the tie-cord and the bag closed over his head like a White Cap's hood.

Checking himself in one of the hallway's gilded mirrors, he had to smile. Both his eyes appeared in one thin slit. His mouth was a small black circle.

He pushed Romains' button and heard distant chimes.

Presently a man with a shaggy blond haircut and pocked cheeks opened the door the length of a safety chain.

"Well, you're obviously not Mr. Toy," he observed. "Who are you, uh, masked stranger?"

Berryman laughed behind the bag. "I'd like it if you never had to see my face," he said in a slightly muffled voice. "I'm Berryman. Ben Toy is away on other business for me."

"I suppose," the forger Romains said. He slid away the gold chain. "I understood he wasn't playing with a full deck myself."

"Where'd you hear that one?"

"From a man. Someone," the forger said.

The living room Berryman entered was large and sunken. It was cluttered with hundreds of lithographs, some stacked against walls like discount art stores. Berryman unsuccessfully tried to take it all in without the aid of peripheral vision.

Romains led him to a white café table. The table overlooked the East River and an immense neon soda sign.

"You wish to exchange pleasantries?" the forger acted belligerent. But there was absolutely no expression on his puffy face. His eyes were sad and rheumy as a chicken's.

Berryman shook his head. He barely looked at Romains. Mostly he examined the Hellgate Bridge. Then he started to explain what he wanted.

"First," he said. "There will be three separate driver's licenses from three southern states. Georgia. South Carolina. Not Tennessee."

The forger made a one-word notation.

"Second. There will be credit cards under the names on the licenses. At the very least, I want Diner's Club and BankAmericard." These two, Berryman knew, were the simplest to fraud.

"Finally," Berryman said. "At least one of the credit cards must carry my photograph. The bank card, I suppose."

M. Romains made a rigid chimneystacked steeple of his fingers and felt-tipped pen. He smiled. "Photograph, Mr. Berryman?"

Berryman withdrew an envelope packet from his jacket.

Romains removed the photo, holding it carefully by its edges. It showed a whisky-nosed man with a blond crew cut. Middle-aged. This, he was certain, was not a Thomas Berryman he would recognize. "Of course." He made another notation. "A photograph on one of the credit cards. A wise safeguard against theft."

"There won't be any problem?" Berryman asked.

The forger looked into the slit of eyes. "No problem," he said. "You must tell me when, and where they must be delivered. I'll tell you how much. Yes?"

Thomas Berryman withdrew another envelope and handed over the fifteen fifty-dollar bills.

Romains counted the bills and nodded. "Good," he smiled. "One half in advance is my requirement."

Now Berryman smiled. "No, my friend," he said. "I'm trusting you with the full payment now. I'll expect delivery in no more than four days," he said. He told the forger where the materials were to be sent.

After leaving the forger's building, Berryman walked up East End Avenue. He turned up 89th Street, walking very slowly to the Flower & Toy Shop. He passed six or eight young people circling around a dead man lying in his black raincoat on the sidewalk. Flies were buzzing over the man's face and a psycho-looking girl was shooing them away with a *New York Times*.

Birds and old men, Berryman thought, die terrible deaths in New York. Much worse than anything he would allow.

• • •

The color of most of the flowers was perfect, but every one of them was dead. Berryman could see that no one had been in the shop for weeks.

Long flowers were hung craze-jane over plastic vases and pots; or they'd just lain down and died in their little wooden windowboxes. Shorter flowers were fallen in heaps, as if they'd been mowed.

The more fragrant flowers (stocks, some roses) gave off a heavy odor; and there was foul water in the room. But most of the dead flowers bore no smell.

Berryman slowly walked up the aisle, breaking flower heads off and smelling them. A hanging lightbulb was on, shining over the counter. Bells on the front door were still jingling back and forth, back and forth.

"Hey Ben," he called out. "Benboy. Goddamnit, Ben."

The answer was *ka-rot, ka-rot*. His boots on the wooden planks.

There was no one in the small back room of the shop either. Water was dripping on more dead flowers in a stainless steel sink. Dead flowers were in a garbage pail. Dead flowers were wrapped in gift paper and ribbons, and signed with various billets doux.

Berryman sat down and composed his own note. He wrote:

> *Ben,*
>   *You're getting crazier than a shithouse rat. Call me on the Island or I'll have to kick your ass.*

He Scotch-taped the note on the inside glass of the front door. It looked like a closed-because-of-a-death-in-the-family notice.

For a very few moments outside, Berryman had a nervous tic in one eye. His mind was flooded with memories that portended (if one *believed*, in one way or another) big trouble for two reverse ass-kissers who had gone against near everything and everybody. Who had stoned girls and fucked Texas boys and cows.

Hampton Bays, June 23

It rained for several days straight near the end of June. It got muddy all around Berryman's home, with the sea smelling extra salty, and all the cloth furniture cool and damp to the touch.

Berryman took the occasion to relax. He needed to relax totally before starting for Tennessee.

Now and then he caught a fish in the ocean; ate it, or threw it back. He thought that the ocean was profoundly intelligent, but that bluefish were not. He kept expecting Ben Toy to pop up, dirty and long-whiskered like some male dog on the bum.

One morning he sat sipping a mug of Yuban and munching honey cakes on the back (beach) porch. It was 9 A.M., but dark, and the house lights were on. He rocked on the love seat (cool on the back of his legs and against his arms), and he read Jimmie Horn's fat autobiography: it was called *Jiminy*.

He read every word, and enjoyed each sentence, each little vignette, immensely. Finishing one page, he would think about what had been described so adroitly, feel bad that it was over, then only slowly move on and start another page.

Over his head the rain sounded as if it was falling on soggy paper. The sky was steamy and cardboard-colored. All vertical noise was the ocean, which seemed especially wet because of the rain and wind.

It was his last pleasant memory of the sea captain's house.

While he sat rocking, reading, humming, Oona came out in a boy's yellow slicker and matching hat.

"What object—that is now sitting in the village of Hampton Bays—would make your day a little brighter?"

Berryman could think of nothing but the newspaper.

Oona told him that she was going to get wine; beef; corn on the cob (did he like corn on the cob? *yes, about hall a dozen at a sitting*); mushrooms; clams (did he like Little Neck clams? *yes, about a dozen at a sitting*).

She waded off through the mud in high, open-heeled sandals. Chose the best mudder, the Cadillac. Waved in the arc cleared by *swish-swash* windshield wipers. Rolled away into the stew.

Berryman drifted back into his book. It was going to be a terrific day, he thought. He was extremely comfortable, content, and Oona was getting to be a genuine delight to be with.

He read. Peacefully inhaled and exhaled the slightly mildew air. Until he was distracted by a sudden loud whacking in the house. It was a cracking whack. Then a pause. Then a whack. A pause.

Berryman slowly walked back through the long hall. The noise got louder. He went through the living room, stopped, switched off a lamp. He took a revolver from the desk. Put it down as a gesture connected with incipient craziness. Picked it up again and slipped it under his T-shirt. He went on to the still-breakfast-warm kitchen. More honey buns were sitting out. More coffee.

The screen door suddenly swung all the way to the outside wall. Hit it. Then swung back with a cracking whack.

As Berryman went to latch the door against the wind, he found a note. The door's hook had been pierced through it.

> TomTom
> Garden spot of the world. You're crazier.
> Can't go killing—killing Jimmie Horn.
> Bigben

Oona came home singing Carly Simon hits— "Anticipation" and "Mockingbird." She was carrying too much groceries for two people. Too many newspapers for five Berrymans.

She found a rained-on copy of *Jiminy* left out on the porch. She called inside and there was no answer.

Without looking further, she sensed that Berryman was gone on business again. This time she thought she knew what the business was.

• • •

Oona stalked around the sea captain's house for the rest of the day.

In a fit of pouting anger she threw the corn, clams and steak out on the lawn.

She broke a living room window that looked out on the empty shore highway. Rain came in on the rug. Wind blew things around the room.

She called up a friend on Cape Cod and another in California. Whenever she hung up the phone, Ben Toy seemed to be calling for Berryman. Finally, she told him to go fuck himself.

The ocean was unseasonably cold that day, fifties, with scary five- and six-foot breakers throwing assorted garbage up on the beach. She sat on driftwood from a big house, boat, big something. Cold foamy water ran around her legs and wet her bottom.

She walked in the ocean, and the first wave that came threw her face-down into the sand. She swallowed salt-water and ate sand.

She walked up the lawn thinking her nose was broken. It wiggled in her fingers. Maybe it always had. She was noticing things. Sand in the spaces between her teeth. The shape of her legs.

Late in the afternoon a peculiar orange sun finally broke through the black ceiling of clouds. A seagull sat on a post, waiting for the picture postcard photographer. Oona was both nauseated and hungry.

She picked up one of the filets off the lawn and eventually cooked it. Then she fell asleep before eight. Her dreams were fast motion, then Richard Avedon-type shots of herself and Berryman in assorted cinematic disaster scenes.

She had completely different ideas in the morning.

She cleaned up what she'd broken and had the Jamaican fix whatever he could. She went around the house, each room, and examined things, possessions, in ways she never had before.

She called Berryman's New York number and got a message recorder. "This is uhm Oona," she said. "I'm missing you in H. Ben Toy has been calling. And uh . . . No, that's it," was the recorded message.

Oona Quinn had reasoned that by leaving her in the house, Berryman was making a commitment to her. She decided that she liked him, liked the way he lived. She decided she wanted to hold on to all of it for a while.

But the girl was wrong on almost all counts.

Quogue, June 24

Paul Lasini was so conservative that at twenty-three he thought Frank Sinatra was the greatest singer in the history of the world. The St. John's University law student, appointed to the Village of Quogue police force for the summer, was the last person to see the funniest man in America.

Lasini was eating a Chinese-food dinner when Ben Toy walked into the Quogue police station talking to himself on June the 24th. Lasini laughed.

The courtly blond man looked stoned to him. Stoned ridiculous or blind drunk and in either case, stumble-bumming around the station house in one tennis sneaker and one beach thong. His hair was unruly and tangled. He'd also pissed in his pants. There was a big dark stain covering one leg of his khaki shorts.

"Oona Quinn is my left hand." Ben Toy slobbered his chin as he spoke. "John Harley is my right hand."

"Better sit down before you fall down," Lasini called over advice.

The desk sergeant, a pink and pudgy veteran named Fall, slowly looked up from his *Daily News*. He kept his finger on his place in the baseball box scores, and he squinted a good look at Toy.

"Here! Hey you!" the sergeant yelled without getting up.

Ben Toy in turn spoke to him. "Which is which?" he asked. It was a serious question: like someone asking about the burial of a loved one in a strange country.

Fall got slightly irritated and burped. "What is *what*?" He looked at Lasini. "What the fuck is this guy talking about? What is this shit right at dinnertime?"

Lasini shook his head and whistled into his soda bottle. "Check the footwear," he grinned.

Fall begrudgingly came around in front of his desk. "Who dressed you this morning?" he asked with poker-faced sternness.

"Oona Quinn is my left hand," Ben Toy tried to explain once again. His face was getting panicky. "Harley John is my right hand.

"Pow! Pow! Pow!" he said with a flourish of flailing arms. "Shot'm." He winked with a sane sense of timing.

He began circling around the concrete block room. Trying to get out a cigarette, he proceeded to spill his entire pack in twos and threes. The cigarettes rolled around the linoleum and made letters with one another. "Which is which?" He gritted his teeth a foot from Pauly Lasini's bug eyes. "I'm not fooling around."

The law student said nothing now.

The pudgy sergeant backpedaled behind his desk. His supper got cold.

"Which is which?" Ben Toy shouted. "Which is which? Which is which? Which is which? Which is which?"

This time Lasini gave him his answer. Oona Quinn and Harley John. Left and right.

Toy smiled at Lasini. He unsheathed a long-barreled Mauser from under his shirt. He handed the ass-heavy cannon to the law student, who held it loosely by the butt, like a wet diaper.

"Like this, man." Ben Toy illustrated a proper grip: two hands on the gun, both arms straight, knees bent slightly. Then he casually walked away to a bench and occupied himself with knotting his windbreaker around his waist.

A second law student took two photographs of Ben Toy, and fingerprinted him on an ordinary ink pad.

There was a scuffle in the back room, and Toy cold-cocked Lasini. It was a loud, cracking right fist that broke the law student's jaw in two places.

Toy was a good fighter, aggressive, unafraid of being hit in the face himself. Sergeant Fall clubbed him from behind with a soda bottle.

As they rode with Ben Toy handcuffed between them, Fall and Lasini were all serious business. They conspired in whispers. *Zim zim zim zim zim.*

"Which is which?" Ben Toy checked every five minutes or so.

Pauly Lasini, his lip and cheek discolored, told him wrong answers in retribution for his wound.

"I'd just like you to repeat these simple numbers." The resident on admissions duty spoke to Toy in a semi-darkened examination room. The room was at the far end of a weird underground tunnel, and there was a network of old yellowed pipes over their heads.

"This is a nuthouse." Toy looked around at the walls and X-rays machines. "Good," he said. "I have a chemical imbalance in my brain. You better write that down."

"Frontward and backward," the resident was friendly, but firm. "Listen to the numbers now, Ben. Don't stare at the walls. No numbers on the walls . . . Thank you . . . OK now. 328 . . . 4729."

Ben Toy slapped down his right hand on the meat wrapping paper which covered the examination table. "Which is my right hand?" he asked.

"Forget about your hands," the resident said. "I'll repeat the number for you."

"Two nine," Ben Toy said. "Which is which, you son of a bitch?"

Aboveground, on rolling green lawns, Ben Toy was walked to the maximum security ward by a team of five aides and a doctor. He was put in a seclusion room and placed on constant two-to-one male supervision. For two hours he was put in wet packs; then he was given so much Thorazine he had trouble rolling over on his mattress.

Nursing notes were written for the 11-7 shift:

> . . . Ben T. was admitted in agitated state this eve. Pt. slaps hand flat on mattress and says, "This is Oona Quinn" (or Shepherd, Berryman, Horn, something or other). Pt. then slaps other hand on mattress. Gives it another name (any of the above) . . . Pt. then tests staff on which hand is which. Pt. will stop on request. But starts again within minutes. His span of attention is about 30 sec. Pt. claims to have shot several people. But this is highly unlikely. Knows much about business, and he may be a flipped-out businessman. Pt. slept well.

In the morning, all of the nursing reports were read and noted by Doctor Alan Shulman.

Oona Quinn was reached that afternoon at Berryman's telephone number. She explained that she hadn't been shot by Ben Toy. She admitted knowing him and said she would like to come talk with him. He was her friend's friend.

She said that no, she didn't know two other friends or business acquaintances of Toy's—neither Harley Wynn nor James Horn. She didn't know anything about them.

Hampton Bays, July 24

I couldn't take my eyes off Oona Quinn.

She was locking up Berryman's house, pausing in front of the door. Then she dropped the keys in her big western saddlebag purse. She had on a navy skirt that day, puffy white blouse, makeup: it was the look of a New York career girl.

I was on my way back to Tennessee for a while. She was going to New England. (To visit friends on Cape Cod, she said. Maybe to stop off at Revere.) We'd decided to go to the airport together.

The Pinto was sputtering badly on the quiet country road that goes out to the Long Island Expressway.

"How long do you plan to be up there?" I asked over the engine noise.

"Dunno," she said. "Haven't figured it out yet. Dunno."

I hesitated before continuing. She was in one of her spacy moods. Continually brushing black hair back out of her face.

"I just want to say one more thing. Serious thing," I said. "I've got to follow through," I started, then stopped. "This kind of reporting . . ."

Oona stopped me. "I'm fine," she said. "You were fine, Ochs. Just do your job."

I started combing my hair with my fingers again. I'm just too big and clumsy to finesse apologies, I was thinking. I don't want to destroy this young woman's life, I was thinking.

We eventually were approaching the one-story concrete building where the Eastern shuttle to Boston leaves.

Oona stayed inside the car for an extra minute and all the N.Y. cabbies started honking at us. Some brutalized dispatcher rapped my window with his newspaper.

When she did get out of the car, she was banging a big, clumsy portmanteau all over her ankles. I thought that the hard square box looked a lot closer to her parents' style than Thomas Berryman's.

Oona disappeared inside the terminal without looking back.

It seemed to me that she'd had enough. I was certain Frank and Margaret Quinn had . . . so I made an executive decision in front of the airways building. I decided to give the family a false name in any stories I'd write. I invented the "Quinn" for them.

That's what some people call protecting a source. It's what I call common decency. And I think it's what Walter and Edna Jones, way back in little, antiquated Zebulon, Kentucky, call "refined."

PART IV

The First Southern Detective Story

Nashville, Early September

It was getting to be election time when I finally settled back into the South. Nashville was still green, and quite beautiful. Her skies were autumnal blue, filled with Kentucky bluebirds. It was what they used to call Indian Summer.

I'd been to five states plus the District of Columbia since July 9th. I'd traveled to New York, Massachusetts, Pennsylvania, Washington, and Texas.

I felt I nearly had my story. I also had a frizzy honey-colored beard. The beard frightened old southern women, small children, and my editors.

Small Problems:

The old biddies on our street insisted I had run away from my family for the several weeks I'd been away. They'd hatched a spellbinding plot in which I'd been fired, then passed the summer bumming my way around the eastern racetrack circuit. One fat Letitia Mills asked me if I thought I was going to find my identity or some damn fool thing like that. I could only answer her in pig Latin. And she could only tip her little black-veiled hat at me. That's their way of saying *fuck you, Charlie*!

The *Citizen-Reporter* wanted my free time. All of it. They said I was up for a senior editor's job because of my fine Berryman stories. My two-hundred-sixty-dollar-a-week salary was raised to three-twenty-five, and I immediately bought a silver Audi Fox.

My lawn hadn't been cut for months; leaves lay piled nigh under higher weeds.

The screen windows were still up.

The screen doors.

The broken hammock.

Larger Problems:

My wife Nan was nervous and edgy.

She wanted to know if I was happy now and I told her *no*, but I was preoccupied. She read the New York notes and didn't react as much as I needed her to. She was taking a karate class at Nashville Free University, and she kept threatening to break things. She liked the new Audi, however.

The kids had forgotten exactly how I fit into the family. They didn't know the man behind the red-blond beard very well. They kept singsonging for me to "take it all off," and that "Gillette was one blade better than whatever I was using." Sometimes I'd get one or both of them down on the floor, rub my beard on their bare bellies, and they'd laugh like hell.

Cat was entering fourth grade and she was involved in the school-busing trouble. She wanted to know if *I* wanted her to ride for an hour and a half back and forth to school every day. She kept telling me about friends who were going to the Baptist Academy.

My younger girl, Janie, was beginning to talk like southern boys. She said that segregation killed piss out of her.

As things turned out, I had to set up an unusual schedule at the newspaper.

I wrote early in the morning (like 5 until 9); and I took leisurely late-night drives to pivotal book locations. In between, I spent my time mending fences and relationships.

Nashville was quiet those days. The election, especially, was subdued.

Both *The Banner* and *Tennessean* were priming up for the investigation of ex-Governor Johnboy Terrell.

I wrote occasional pretrial articles, but in the main—free of newspaper deadlines and space limitations—it was Thomas Berryman.

At this point, I still didn't know what had happened to Berryman after the shooting.

I was to find out that Oona Quinn had misled me slightly. I was to find out quite a lot of nasty little things.

• • •

According to Lewis Rosten, the real Dashiell Hammett/Frederick Forsyth detective story didn't begin until I returned to Nashville.

Six weeks of my life belie the absolute truth of that statement, but Lewis is partially correct.

Over the course of the fall, he and I, and numerous other *Citizen* reporters, compiled over twenty-five hundred pages of notes, interviews, phone numbers, hotel and restaurant receipts, all sorts of trivial documents. We could have done Ph.D. dissertations on any of these four men: Thomas John Berryman, Jefferson John Terrell, Bertram Poole, Joseph Dominick Cubbah.

Lewis was writing a book then too, but he was also being conscientious, even noble, about his city editor responsibilities.

He'd sit around the *Citizen* city room nitpicking some fourteen-year-old farmboy's account of an automobile wreck, then he'd call me at home at twelve midnight, and ask if I'd like to meet him somewhere like Lummie's Heart of Dixie.

"Just to kick around some theories I have about Berryman," he'd always set the hook. "Just for thirty minutes or so, Ochs."

More often than not I'd meet him.

Lummie's Heart of Dixie is a *Citizen-Reporter* lunch bar which is returned to the local, or "real," people after 5 P.M.

From five o'clock on it's crawling with failed country music singers who will slide into your booth and give you a sad song for the price of a Sterling beer. By my standards, it's the best, certainly the cheapest show in town.

By general Tennessee standards though, Lummie's is a talking bar.

Because of my high 6'7" visibility, and my general good-natured laugh, I'm tolerated by the crowd there.

Lewis Rosten, however, can be a wholly different matter.

On account of this, we generally tried to commandeer one of the red vinyl booths near the rear exit. It would take us twenty minutes to spread out all our notes and scraps, and they'd cover up every flat space available.

Only then would we begin the ritualistic struggles over what was going where, in which article.

This letter is typical of the kind of notes and scraps we brought to decide what to do with. It had suddenly appeared in my mail slot one Monday in late September:

> Dear Mr. Ochs Jones,
>
> My occupation is customs inspector. I live at Rockaway Beach in the Queens, New York. Recently I read one of your stories about the killer Thomas Berryman in *Parade* magazine. This was the story that ran here on September 7th.
>
> Well, to get to the pernt. At the end of July, I was sent Diner's Club chits for four dinners at the Tale of the Fox restaurant in Nashville, Tennessee. But I had never been to Tennessee, and sure enough, when I check my wallet, no Diner's Card, and a few others missing too.

The forged tabs were forged J.P. Golly, myself, and it wasn't until this month that they were traced to Thomas Berryman. Included on each tab was a listing of the exact meals which might be of interest to your files.

1 Vodka Gimlet
1 Sirloin
1 Black coffee

I even started to picture this character, this elegant pickpocket, settling down to these cute little dinners. On yours truly!

Anyways, I don't know what this information is worth to you, but I don't think I should be the one to pay for the dinners.

John Patrick Golly
GS-11

• • •

The funny (peculiar) thing was that J.P. Golly had already been recompensed for his losses by Diner's Club. The *Citizen-Reporter* wasn't about to pay him, of course, but we checked with Diner's anyway.

Rosten and I checked *everything* that could humanly be checked.

• • •

Moses Reed had written an editorial about Jimmie Horn the day after Horn's election in 1970. An immediate public opinion poll was taken on the piece's merits, and the side and rear windows of Reed's Country

Squire were subsequently broken by men and boys with Louisville Sluggers.

The editorial had begun:

> IN HIS CHILDHOOD PHOTOGRAPHS, JIMMIE LEE HORN, A SQUARE-JAWED CASSIUS CLAY PHYSICAL TYPE, LOOKED LIKE A LEADER, AN OBVIOUS, NATURAL-BORN LEADER.
>
> SO TOO, HORN'S EARLY WORK IN THE NASHVILLE SCHOOL SYSTEM BORE OUT THIS FACT.
>
> HAD THIS CITY, THEREFORE, HAD THE FORESIGHT TO SE-LECT HIM FROM AMONG THE CHILDREN GROWING UP AT THAT TIME IN OUR SHANTYTOWN DISTRICT; HAD THIS CITY PUT HORN THROUGH TWENTY-ONE YEARS OF FORMAL SCHOOLING (INCLUDING SEVEN YEARS OF IVY SCHOOLING); HAD THIS CITY GIVEN HIM THE HARDBOUND EDITION OF OLIVER WENDELL HOLMES WHICH HE BOUGHT FOR HIMSELF UPON HIS VALE-DICTORY AT PEARL HIGH SCHOOL; HAD THIS CITY GROOMED THIS OBVIOUSLY SPECIAL NATURAL RESOURCE, AS IF IT WAS DESTINED TO BECOME SOMETHING OTHER THAN A BUS STA-TION REDCAP—
>
> —HAD WE FINE CITIZENS OF NASHVILLE DONE ALL, OR IN-DEED ANY OF THESE THINGS—THEN, WE WOULD HAVE SOME WAY OF UNDERSTANDING WHAT HAS HAPPENED HERE THIS WEEK.
>
> BUT AS WE DID NONE OF THESE THINGS FOR JIMMIE LEE HORN, SINCE WE IN FACT CONSPIRED TO RETARD HIS DEVEL-OPMENT, WE ARE A CITY IN SHOCK TODAY. WE ARE IN SHOCK, AND MANY OF US ARE IN SHAMEFUL AWE AT THE WAY JIMMIE HORN HAS COME UP OUT OF SHANTYTOWN, AND BECOME OUR MAYOR, AS WELL AS EVERYTHING ELSE HE IS TODAY . . .

I personally got to know Horn and his family fairly well after his election in '70.

Since that may sound like false modesty coming from a man who won prizes writing about him, I should say that Horn had the most elaborate set of defenses I've ever seen any man build around himself.

Not the least of these defenses was a quick, joking manner that had led some other reporters to create a media myth that Horn was just a "happy-go-lucky nigger."

I don't believe Horn was a happy man at all. In fact, that's one thing I'm fairly certain of. He was a driven man. He had conditioned himself to be a successful black leader and a spokesman. That was his life. With the exception of a few unguarded moments (and those usually had an ulterior purpose), I never saw what I would characterize as the *private man* in Jimmie Horn.

Over the years though, I built up a collection of tapes on the *public man*: on Horn the thinker, the writer, the bull-thrower.

Jimmie Horn Speaking on Jim Crow:

"Just after Vietnam got important, in 1967, my youngest brother's best friend—he was a veteran, and also an Esso gas-pump jockey—was fished out of the Cumberland River with his testicles in the pockets of his bluejeans.

"You see, he'd been gossip-associated with a white woman. More than that, he'd been loving her regularly.

"So now, we come to the middle 1970s. And now, barring some unforeseen and unlikely event, the pundits say I could become one of Tennessee's senators. Just like it was Massachussetts down here.

"Well, I don't know about that. I don't know if anything has changed quite like that.

"Jim Crow may be gone, technically, but he's not forgotten."

On Beulahland:

"Believe it or not, I have always embraced the southern values of honor, hospitality, and graciousness.

"I like the way things are up-front down here, much better than I liked it up North.

"A sheriff in Jackson City says, 'The only thing I like better than arrestin' niggers is catchin' a big seven-pound bass.' I like that. I like knowing who is *they* and who is *we*."

On James Earl Ray:

"The damndest pity I know of.

"The entire Memphis court proceedings, following one of the most spectacular and heinous crimes of the century, King's murder in cold blood, took one hundred and forty-four minutes . . . After a little more than three hours, during which no formal legal procedures took place, it was over. There was no cross-examination of James Earl Ray/Galt/St. Vincent Galt/Bridgeman/Sneyd, or anyone else for that matter. It was history as the mosquito bite, the blink of an eye.

"Then, three years ago, after throwing my weight around in some ways I don't care to remember, I got to visit Ray at Bruskey State Prison.

"Ray was wearing a blue jean jacket and work shirt, and he was dusting leaves along a sidewalk. He seemed to me to have the natural look of a groundskeeper.

"We sat down on a front yard bench and for some unknown reason he offered me a cigarette. 'You want to know how I did it, too,' he said.

"No, I told him. I'd like to know who did it.

"Ray smiled and lighted a second cigarette for himself—one already being in his mouth. He puffed on two cigarettes for the next five minutes or so, staring straight at the ground. He said absolutely not one more word. I think he was playing with me.

"For the first time, and I don't know exactly why, I believed that he'd actually done it. I believed that he'd done it for his own personal satisfaction, and I felt he was proud of what he'd done.

"Then recently they moved him to Nashville of all places. He's appealing again. Now nobody believes he did it again."

On a Magazine Article Claiming He'd Read
Amy Vanderbilt *to His Wife*:

"This is true. Last night, in fact, Maureen and I discussed a lesson in etiquette for upwardly mobile black people.

"In the lesson, two up-and-coming black painters, both foremen, are working on a tall building and one of them falls. 'Hey, now, don't fall,' his friend says. 'I can't help it, I already fell,' the falling man answers. 'Well, you're goan fall right on a white lady down there,' the friend comes right back. And that falling man stops falling, and returns to the roof.

"That is etiquette for black people. Just as I read it in Miss Vanderbilt's fine book."

On Being Shot:

"I read that Dr. King thought about it a lot. For him, it seemed to be a means of guaranteeing his legacy. I doubt he looked forward to it, though, as some have written.

"I saw James Meredith get shot in person. Nineteen sixty-six, in Hernando, Mississippi. He was shot in the stomach. He had on a striped short-sleeved shirt and it literally turned red down the front. Meredith crawled to the side of the road on his hands and knees before anyone could help him. It wasn't inspiring for me to watch.

"I'm more fatalistic about it now though. I try to deal with it openly, even within my family. I can joke about it going into some big rally outside of Nashville or out of state. In Nashville itself, I feel pretty safe."

On Fear:

"Fear is the one thing that has kept the blackman down so long in the South.

"My grandmother used to tell us a story—and she was a strict, card-carrying Baptist lady who didn't exaggerate, much less lie—she said that in plantation days, the people were so terrified of whites that they put their heads in cooking pots or the wood stove before they would dare to pray out loud.

"I remember too, there was always this phrase around when I was growing up—'What if the white people find out?'

"And that's why, above all, a black leader cannot show fear . . . Of course I'm a lot braver with my thirty-seven-year-old body than I was with the one I had when I was twenty-five or so. (Laughs.) You know me, Ochs."

But I didn't really know him. Not really.

Nashville, June 25

Marblehead Horn, a sentimental small businessman (greengrocer), had cultivated four, proud, jungle-thick inches of hair directly over his son's skull. He cared for it like a private gardener for thirteen years, then gave his young son the choice of whether or not to keep it. Jimmie Horn kept it.

This haircut wasn't the modern, natural look, but an old-time style from the early days of Reconstruction Nashville. From the unpromised land days just before Tennessee passed the very first of the Jim Crow laws. It was near the shape of a kidney bean; but singular-looking; and somewhat impressive on Jimmie.

People generally liked "the burr," as it was called. I did.

One eastern political consultant named Santo Massimino didn't like it at all. He told Jimmie it would lose him all of eastern Tennessee, and he was right. He asked him to get it barbered before he started his campaign for the United States Senate. He assured the mayor that he knew how hard it would be for him, and Jimmie Horn assured him that he didn't know any such thing.

● ● ●

Barber Robinson was cute in a bizarre way. Like an old, old blackbird, close up, with its little gray-black crew cut.

He played his razor strap with an ancient but gleaming straight razor. He rocked the spindly knees lost somewhere in his baggy trousers. Gummed his old yellowbone teeth over and over. "Yesss indeedee," he finally spoke. "My main baby is back in Nigeria."

Jimmie Horn smiled a crooked smile and slapped the old-timer's butt as they passed like familiar dancing partners in midshop. "Your baby is getting old before his time." The mayor affected another friendly grin. "I have gray hair . . . uh," he was setting up a punch line or sad truth, "on my balls."

The old man roared and tossed his little head back as an afterthought. "If you be old, Jimmie Horn, I mus' be daid."

He hustled over to his money drawer, and brought back shiny black-handled scissors to trim the mayor's hair. He smiled with his tiny black-bird's head low to the red leather of the barber's chair. "Regular trim?"

Horn shook the burr in reply. He fluttered his lips. He coughed into his fist. "Have you ever heard," he asked the old man, "of a political consultant?"

Barber Robinson gave the question some thought. "Nuh, I haven't," he finally concluded.

Rarely looking up, preferring to watch ambitious weevils crawl walls in a lidded mayonnaise jar, the mayor told his barber about Santo Massimino's request.

When the "bulljive" was completed, Horn watched the barber shuffle away to sit in a straight-backed chair by the door. He looked out to the street. He looked over the backs of two autographed photos of Horn on display in his front window. Over the back of an old Vitalis poster. Over a new Afro-sheen one. And a new red, white, and blue basketball reputedly autographed by the Memphis Tams.

The old man relit a Camel stub off his countertop and smoked as if it was stinging him.

Potbellied little boys were playing stickball past his face out the door. It was buggy summer. Jimmie Horn thought that the feel of the room was like a veterans' hospital.

Rubbing his palm back and forth over his short peppercorn hair, the old man said, very softly, "Shee-it." Then, flicking his butt to the middle of the dirt sidewalk, he said, "Fuck me in the rear end."

Still ignoring the mayor, shaking to the naked eye, the old barber stood rigidbacked and began patting talcum powder up and down his skinny, knobbed arms. He started another Camel.

Then quickly saved it, back on the counter by the Morobine. He carefully turned on the Zenith and the protruding orange tubes blinked, blinked, then caught.

He swiped at a pin-striped bib and faced the mayor with a fierce, smothering look about his eyes. With redness and tears. "Shee-it in my pants," he said.

Jimmie Horn nodded. Then he looked straight ahead at the chalky mirror.

He saw the burr. The familiar, friendly burr. Not a kidney bean. Not a vote obstructor.

He recalled photographs featuring the burr. Reflections of it. Its shadow at night: his furry hat.

Like some careless hedgecutter, the old barber came head and shoulders into the mirror and lopped a chunk off the tall, revered pompadour. "Stand out like a diamon' in a goat's ass," was the comment.

Horn accepted his punishment without flinching. Without words. Stoical as Aurelius, whom he admired when he was tired or sleepy, he watched his own stone-face in the mirror.

"No way," the barber sang an old tired-voiced tune, "no way you was gonna lose election, baby. Hundred percent black people's cooperation." He yanked a strip of hair away that left Jimmie Horn nearly bald in one spot.

With that the mayor brought both his dark eyes to the right, to Robinson's eyes. "Be careful," he warned in his soft, firm voice. "You are Jimmie Horn's barber. You pay attention to your work."

The old barber took his message and there was a brief silence.

"Come brand new into this town," he resumed his speech with a new cutting angle. "Massomino or which-what. Says hop to Jimmie Horn. And Jimmie Horn hop. He hop right exactly to."

"I have my reasons." Horn finally found himself at the point of apologies. "You don't get to see everything that goes on . . . uh . . . It's complicated. Just cut my hair, please, Robbie."

The old man slashed down on one fuzzy sideburn. Then he got the other one. "What're you doin' to us baby?" he started crying. "I don't like this. Understand it . . ."

Jimmie Horn drifted into a Sunoco parking lot with a popped-up Spaulding outside in the street. Into the alleys of an urban renewal project. He drifted in his own sports memories. Drifted in memories of solemn old men and women giving him dreamy, semi-lucid talkings-to. Asking him if he knew that he was smart enough to go off to Tennessee Agricultual Industrial one day?

The old man started in with his sharp straight razor. "You know they gonna kill Henry Aaron yet. You know that," he said. "I dream that."

"You know I'm just your dumb baby," Jimmie Horn answered with his eyes closed. Feeling hot lather on his throat, lots of hot lather. "No common sense," he smiled, teeth whiter than the shaving cream.

"Don't you smile at me like that," the old man was strong on top of his blade. "I know that one other dumb baby." *Scrape. Scrape. Scrape.* "He smiled. Played his piano so pretty he got his fingers broke in a car hood. And that pretty Carma. She smiled too. Dumb happy baby. Shot her with women's stockings over their heads." *Scrape. Scrape.*

Scrrrr-ape. Scrape. Scrape. Scrape. Scrape. "Finished."

Jimmie Horn opened his eyes and took a good look at himself in the mirror. Something in his mind said *frown*, but he didn't.

"This is good," he patted the shrunken head. "You've done it." He grinned so convincingly that the old man took pleasure. "Saved me."

But Jimmie Horn was singing a different tune to himself. *Like a diamond in a goat's ass*, he repeated. *You are exactly right, old wise man.*

Horn drove the city's Oldsmobile back toward downtown Nashville. He followed Church Street to 6th, then switched over to West End Avenue. It was 8:15 on the clock outside Morrison's Cafeteria and he still had some work to do. It was something he had little stomach for, but it had to be done anyway.

Jimmie Horn flicked the car's noisy directionals on, then waited his turn to go into the parking lot flanking Nashville Police Headquarters.

• • •

Police Interrogation Room #3 had a small square window up too high to be reached without a stepladder. There were three orange plastic chairs. A copper doorknob.

Everything else was white.

Two very black blackmen, Marshall "Cottontail" Hayes and Vernon Hudson, sat facing each other in two of the chairs.

Hudson, thirty-seven years old, wore a short-collar white shirt, blue bus-driver's tie, gray pants. He also had a brown shoulder holster setup over his arm. Hayes, aged twenty, was dressed in dark burgundy and gold: a feathered burgundy hat, silk jumpsuit, calfskin boots, a variety of gold bracelets, rings, and earrings.

One thing was obvious in the small room: Cottontail Hayes hadn't learned how to dress in his hometown of Gray Hawk, Mississippi.

Jimmie Horn was standing in the room, directly behind Hayes. Occasionally the twenty-year-old would look over his shoulder at the mayor, but Horn never returned the look.

"I understand you murdered a man name of Freddie Tucker." Vernon Hudson spoke in a surprisingly soft voice.

Silence.

"I also understand you the big new dope man around town," Hudson said.

Silence. This time Hayes slowly stroked his long goatee.

Jimmie Horn sat down in the third chair. He looked into Hayes' face.

Hayes examined what he thought to be an imperfection in one of his rings.

Horn lighted up a Kool and handed it across to the boy. "I'd like to explain something to you," he said.

Cottontail Hayes accepted the cigarette. He touched it to his lips and took small, feminine puffs. His bracelets jingled.

"There's a trick for a black man being mayor," Horn said.

"Of course," Hayes nodded. He smiled like he was hip to the whole situation.

"The trick to a black man being mayor," Jimmie Horn continued, "is that you cannot afford a single fuck-up blackman in the community. Because white people will only blow up what they do, blow it way out of proportion. They'll talk about a murder, or a mishandled welfare case, like it's the rule rather than the exception."

Hayes shook out his bracelets at Jimmie Horn. "Listen, I don' have time for this shit, you know. Where's my fucking lawyer at?"

After Hayes spoke his line, Jimmie Horn stood up again. He walked across the room and left it.

"Jackass," he said to himself outside. He started down a long pale green corridor with cork bulletin boards covered with official and unofficial public notices. The corridor emptied into a small waiting room with a lot of plastic chairs lined up by a table surface completely covered by magazines. Not an inch of the tabletop was visible, Horn noticed. He was trying to calm himself down.

An attractive black girl was sitting alone in the room.

She had on expensive green velvet pants, hoop earrings, platform shoes. She was smoking like a 1950s movie queen, and Horn was tempted to tell her to stop it. She was Marshall Hayes' woman. Eighteen years old.

Then she was talking to him in a loud voice. "Where is the Cottontail?" she asked. "We got to go."

Horn sat down in one of the plastic chairs. He had a Kool. "If you don't go away from that man," he found himself saying to the girl, "you'll be dead before you're twenty-five years old."

That was all. Then he was walking back to Room #3 again.

Hayes was down on the white floor; he was clutching his stomach as though something was going to fall out if he let it go. Vernon Hudson was holding the feathered burgundy hat.

"You've been selling cocaine, and you've been selling heroin here," Horn began to talk before the door was closed. "You've sold heroin to freshmen and sophomores at Pearl High School."

"I never sol' no fuckin heh-rehn in my fuckin life."

Horn bent over so that his face was only a foot above that of Hayes.

"Listen brother, *you have sold heroin*. You've sold plenty of heroin. People sell heroin for you. If there was the slightest doubt about that I would not be here. I don't play games."

"So how come you here?" Hayes' voice shot an octave higher than he'd wanted.

"I'm here to throw you out of this town. Plain and simple."

"What, man, you can't do shit like that."

"Brother," Horn was using the word to deride, "I can do anything I damn well please. This is my town. Not the east side, or the west side, or Church Street. The whole goddamn thing!"

"And if you are seen in it after tonight," Vernon Hudson spoke calmly from over near the door, "I will shoot you and swear before the judge that you had a gun . . . In case you hadn't heard, boy, they shoot niggers down here."

Jimmie Horn started to leave the room, then he stopped in the open door.

"Marshall Hayes," he sighed, "I'm sorry to have to do this to you." He started to say more, but then he just closed the door on the man.

He left the building using a way that avoided the teenage girl waiting for Cottontail Hayes. Then, at 10:30 P.M., the mayor of Nashville headed home.

His car was followed by a green Dodge Polara.

New York, June 24, 25

Thomas Berryman was meanwhile eating a special diet of spaghetti and draft beer.

He did this for three consecutive days so that his face grew puffy. His stomach spread. He put on twenty pounds and ten years, and began to resemble the picture on M. Romains' BankAmericard.

One day in the last week in June he got a dollar crew cut in a subway station barber shop. He had his mustache shaved for another thirty-five cents. Then he purchased a baggy, pea green suit in Bond's with the BankAmericard.

To loosen himself up that same night, he traveled to Shea Stadium with a Soho artiste who used eye shadow and rouge to make herself look like Alice Cooper; who liked to do *anything, everything, just something different, real.*

Berryman masqueraded as "the Pleasure King." He wore dark glasses and a black muscle shirt with his crew cut. The two of them obliterated themselves in the right field bleachers. They ate hot franks, drank Schaeffer beer, and smoked pot as the Red Sox bombarded the Yanks three hundred thirty-one to a hundred-nineteen.

In the morning, Thomas Berryman caught a businessman's flight to Nashville. It was his thirtieth birthday and he was daydreaming about spending year thirty-one in retirement at Cuernavaca or San Miguel de Allende in Mexico. Strangely, it was near the kind of dream (dream/game plan/ambition) Harley Wynn had once nurtured.

Berryman was aware of two strong inclinations regulating his entire life.

The first was the work of his circuit judge father, and it involved doing things well. It was reflex, Pavlovian:

when Thomas Berryman did something to perfection, he derived a satisfying pleasure from the action. Doing things well, anything at all, was compulsive with Berryman.

The second inclination came from his mother's part of the family. Berryman thought of it as his "country gentleman" side. He'd first taken this second urge seriously, as seriously as the first urge, in 1971. He was working in Mexico when it happened.

Señor Jorge Amado Marquez's hacienda was located some ninety miles west of Mexico City. It was a labyrinth of white stucco rooms, newer flamingo pink stables, and green-as-your-garden fences and railings. It was situated on a deep blue lake like Italy's Como, looking straight up at a small volcano.

Jorge Marquez was living alone on the huge estate in 1971.

His wife had died mysteriously that year (a self-inflicted gunshot while out in a family motorboat). His daughter was living with a photographer in Mexico City, a handsome, high-pompadoured man who would have been perfect for Costa-Gavras movies.

Jorge Marquez had invited Berryman to stay with him for the week before he would do his work. As the particular job was a simple one, automatic, Berryman had entertained his whims for gracious living, and accepted the invitation.

He'd slept in a third-floor suite equipped with a wraparound terrace some seventy-five feet over the lake. The front windows looked over at the volcano. A large back window looked out on bush country· brazil-wood and palms, streaming with parrots.

In the early morning, dark-haired thirteen- and fourteen-year-old girls would be out on his terrace from sometime before sunrise. They were pretty little girls with dusty brown legs. They played silent barefoot games until Berryman came to the door leading out onto the terrace. Then, giggling, blushing, curtsying like the maids in American movies, the pubescent señoritas would bring him bananas, papaya, mangos; bacon, whitefish from Lake Chapala.

His afternoons could be peaceful sailing out and around the volcano; swimming in lake water clear enough to see bottom whenever it hadn't rained; hunting deer with or without Marquez, who was gentleman enough to give Berryman his choice.

Finally, the evenings would consist of large dinner parties or less formal cookouts. At those, Berryman would be introduced as an American businessman connected with Marquez' tin and banana conglomerate. American women and wealthy, cosmopolitan señoritas would attend these parties, and in the mornings, the teenage Mexican girls would get to secretly examine these women from Berryman's terrace.

When the week ended, Thomas Berryman held the firm idea that he would soon try Mexican life again. For the moment though, Marquez' business was on.

Riding in a coughing, gasping native bus, he traversed Route 14 to Mexico City one afternoon. Some tinkling burros outside kept pace with the bus, but he was in no real hurry.

Once inside Mexico City, he exchanged his country whites for dusty huaraches and bluejeans. He moved into a hostel for students and teachers, and began to wear silver wirerim eyeglasses.

The first two evenings there were spent carousing with carefree students from the University of Wisconsin and their quiet, homosexual advisor. Berryman became known as a high school teacher from Westchester in New York.

Late in his third afternoon in Mexico City, however, Berryman stole a gray pickup truck. The truck was full of goats, chickens, and a few squealing pigs. The truck was heavy of itself, yet Berryman found it could get up to seventy miles per hour with not too much strain.

During that evening, the gray truck was seen several times parked in, and driving around, the Plaza de la Constitucion.

Slightly before midnight, it struck the Costa-Gavras photographer head-on in a narrow, one-way street; it was moving at nearly fifty-five miles per hour at the time.

The Marquez girl's lover had had a high wet-looking pompadour and flashing white teeth that stood out in the dark. Even that was more than Thomas Berryman wanted to know about him. He preferred to store memories from his week with Señor Marquez. Dwelling on the other thing was self-defeating.

• • •

An elderly woman, a southern woman, tapped at Berryman's arm and he slowly removed his Braniff Airlines stereo earphones.

She wanted her seat moved back, which was fine, but she also wanted to talk about her recently deceased son-in-law. "Michael was only fifty-eight," she said. "Michael has two lovely daughters at Briarcliff. Michael had been planning to retire in just five years . . ."

Berryman occasionally glanced away from the woman; he saw the beginnings of Nashville out the window.

The fasten seatbelts order was given. The earphones were collected.

Berryman found himself taking a deep breath. Examining his clothes in relation to the dress of the southern businessmen on board.

When the front door stewardess welcomed crew-cut Thomas Berryman "home," he smiled like a goat, and spoke perfect southern to her.

Carrying his small, black leather bag across the airfield's landing tarmac, Berryman thought of it this way: he was just making a stopover on his way back to Mexico.

Nashville, June 26

On the second Tuesday before the Fourth, Berryman came out the electric doors of the Farmer's Market with a milkbottle quart of orange juice and a pound of Farmwife powdered doughnuts. He was wearing khaki pants, a wrinkled Coca-Cola shirt with the sleeves rolled up over his biceps; and he was a dead ringer for a Tennessee redneck. In his body, and in his mind.

He sat down on the warm hood of his Hertz Ford Galaxie, fingered the milkbottle Braille, and admired Nashville women doing their thing: shopping. He ate several of the warm doughnuts, which were nice, even sitting on hot metal.

As usual, his independence delighted him: it was 11 A.M. and his job for the day was easy, with high pay.

Traffic was light through the early afternoon. It was a day of one-bag pickups.

There were occasional gypsy bands, excellent wives nonetheless, in curlers, with their kerchiefs puffed high over their foreheads like birdcages. There were childlike old men, in aloha sport shirts, with baggy trousers belted high around their waists like mailbags.

Sometimes Berryman would strike up conversation with one or the other. But in the main, he kept his eye on two Amos 'n' Andy Negro carpenters handcrafting a platform stage in the middle of the parking lot. Jimmie Horn would speak from the platform.

Berryman sat on the Ford. Then he walked the perimeter of the airfield-sized market lot.

He visited a few Plaza shops. Bought a J.C. Penney olive shirt and tie to clash with his Bond's suit. Watched a policeman reading a comic book in a patrol car.

There was a thirty-gauge shotgun propped up facing the windshield in the front seat.

Around lunchtime he sat under a Cinzano umbrella outside of Lums, and he sipped Cinzano at the urging of a waitress named D. Dusty.

(Afterward, she remembered him.)

Across a narrow arcade, the Farmer's Market roof was long, flat, pitch tar. It got hot and gooey by midafternoon. The tar oozed at the edges of the gutter.

The building's front facade, a red-on-royal-blue sign, rose about three feet higher than the roof itself. The roof's backside was hanging in the woods. Magnolias. A thick green wall from the loading platform all the way out to Route 95 eastbound to Knoxville.

Puffing on a cigarillo, Thomas Berryman took in every detail.

As he was about to leave, Berryman saw a long-haired boy he'd noticed two or three times earlier that day.

The boy was tall and skinny, wearing green army fatigues and smoked brown glasses. His hair was curly and he made Berryman think of Oliver Twist.

He'd been sitting at a bus stop. He'd been trying to make time with a little black waitress in Lums. Now he was sadsacked on the whitestone sidewalk in front of the market itself. He was watching the two black carpenters.

Berryman made a mental note of the boy, then called it a day. On a per diem basis he had made over twenty thousand dollars.

Nashville, June 27

"By the selected day," Ben Toy had told me, "Berryman will have one plan he thinks is 100% foolproof. And if he doesn't think his plan is 100%, he'll walk away from the job. He did that with Jesse Jackson in Chicago. He likes challenges, but his challenges are in the figuring."

Sitting in my workroom, thinking about Ben Toy again, one thing struck me that should have been clear to me before. Toy had hated Thomas Berryman. I wasn't so sure that he knew he did, but I was sure that he hated him.

On the 27th day of June, Berryman shut himself in his hotel room, room 4H, from six to six; he studied Jimmie Horn's known daily routines like a Talmudist.

Berryman's hotel was a double-building rooming house in the hospital district west of West End Avenue in Nashville. It was called the Claremont, and had a big sign on the porch: HOME COOKED MEALS FOR LADIES AND GEN-TLEMEN. Every afternoon at the Claremont the regular boarders could be viewed in the lobby, eating mint ice and Nabiscos, watching the soaps or a baseball game. A room there cost Berryman $26.50 for the week.

For his efforts that first morning, Berryman learned that Jimmie Horn was careless, but that his aides were not.

That night he actually followed Horn's car from City Hall. The mayor rode with an armed chauffeur and lots of company that evening—a cadre of paranoid white men

who were constantly glancing around each new land-
scape, checking it for danger signs like scared jackrab-
bits. Another car, probably police, a green Dodge, also
followed the Horn vehicle.

Horn's little girl met the car at the head of the driveway,
and he got out and walked with her to the main house.
Their arm-in-arm walk was easily five hundred yards and
Berryman wondered if they did it every night. The car
went on ahead. The Dodge parked near the front gates.

Looking on through roadside bramble and an eight-foot
spiked fence, Berryman could hear their footsteps on
gravel. He could also see another police patrolcar parked
in the circular part of the driveway up near the house. *Jesus
Christ*, he was thinking, *they sure watch out for his ass*.

Directly behind him, very close, Berryman heard
bushes crashing down. He turned around to face a tall
state trooper with a mustache.

"You cain't park here," the man stated in a matter-of-
fact drawl. "You want your look at fancy ni-gras, you got
to go to the movies. Move on now, buddy."

"Do that." Berryman grinned as stupidly as he could.
He got up from his knees and fled to his car in a fast duck
waddle. "Yes sir, do that right now," he stammered.
"Damn idle curiosity anyhow."

Once back inside his car, driving down the asphalt
road away from the mayor's mansion, Berryman could
feel blood pounding in his brain. Now Thomas, he was
thinking, you have got to do a whole lot better than that.

Which he did.

Nashville, June 28

Berryman concluded that the New South, the physical plant anyway, was a colossal mistake; it had no personality; it was living-boxes out of 1984 . . . The next morning he was back poring over city maps and other books about Nashville.

He quickly memorized street names, routes, alternate routes, key locations; he tried to get a feel for the city; a basic feel for what happened when he went north, went west, went east.

He wore hornrim eyeglasses and was continually massaging the bridge of his nose. His eyes were sore. He worked right through the cleaning lady.

Study, study, study—and then study some more. *Do it right; perfect your technique.*

After a café lunch of eggs, grits, and tenderloin, Berryman drove and walked around the capitol and business sections of Nashville. He was wearing mirrored sunglasses, a Levi's shirt, cowpuncher jeans.

He thought that downtown Nashville was typical of the New South: it was a small town, with big city pretensions.

The Nashville skyline was a cluster of fifteen-to-twenty-five-story buildings which made Berryman think of a smaller, poorer Houston. The capitol buildings looked like a miniature Washington. A pretzel configuration of parkways added a hint of Los Angeles.

It was a clean city though; and the air was still relatively fresh.

Nashville's rich and poor alike bought their clothes off the rack. The men wore Sears and Montgomery Ward double-knit suits. Most of them wore white patent leather belts and white loafers with golden chains and buttons.

Nashville women still wore short skirts, and stockings. Thigh ticklers and hot pants were on display in all the department and dime store windows.

The southern city was practicing conspicuous consumption, but most of it was being done in Rich's department store and Walgreen's.

To help complete his own ensemble, Berryman stopped in a Kinney's Shoe Store and bought a pair of beige Hush Puppies. They figured to go well with the green suit, and they were also dress shoes he could run in.

The clerk who packaged them looked from sunglasses to shoes, shoes to sunglasses. "Don't look like your type," she said.

"Mos' comf'table walkin' shoe in America," Berryman smiled. It wasn't what you said, it was how you said it.

In the late afternoon, he drove uptown to Horn campaign headquarters. It was located in an unrented automobile showroom on West End Avenue.

Still squinting in the harsh sunlight, he stood outside the storefront and walked its length.

The showroom windows were covered with posters of

Jimmie Horn talking *one on one* with a wide spectrum of people. All of the photographs were striking; Horn apparently had some southern Bruce Davidson following him around with a camera.

There was Jimmie Horn standing on some grassy knoll with a white football coach. Horn with his wife by their kitchen stove. Horn with Howard Baker and Sam Ervin. Horn fishing off some country bridge with an old black grandfather. Horn with Nixon. With Minnie Pearl. With a young vet just arrested for robbing a gas station.

Berryman felt the correct emotion: a warm friendly feeling about Jimmie Horn.

Behind all the photographs, inside the showroom, a gabby campaign worker cheerfully outlined the mayor's Independence Day schedule for Berryman. She sat under a faded Sign of the Cat, talking like a parrot.

"In the early mawnin'," she used a leftover salesman's desk as her lectern, "startin' with a pa-rade at nine, the next senator of Tennessee will appear at a celebrity *Rallie* to be held at Vand-a-bilt Stadium, or rather, Dudley Field.

"Johnny Cash. Albuht Gohr. Kris Kristoffason. They'ahr just a few of the personalities who will be on hand.

"At noon"—she handed Berryman a glossy leaflet entitled *The Dream*—"at noon, there will be a fund-raisin luncheon at Rogah Millah's King of the Road.

"At fohah," she smiled like a mother of the bride, "the mayor will speak to ow-ah black people. This will take place at the Fa'mer's Market.

"At eight. Mayor Horn will appear with Guvnah Winthrop at the new *zoom, zoom, zoom,* Nashville Speedway. This will be ow-ah fawworks show, uh course."

As the ramble continued, the long-haired youth from the Farmer's Market wandered in off West End Avenue. He was wearing the same green fatigues, and close up, Berryman could see he was easily in his mid-twenties.

This was Bert Poole, the divinity student later killed by the gunman from Philadelphia.

"Help you?" the garrulous woman called to him.

Poole didn't answer, or even look up at the voice.

He read some handouts about Horn stacked high on a wooden banquet table. He examined the advertising posters on the walls, and looked at Berryman and the woman with the same critical eye.

Then he popped out the swinging doors, just as quickly as he had come in.

"Comes in here every other day," the gabby woman said to Berryman. "Never answers a civil question. Never smiles. Never volunteers to do a little work."

Berryman watched as Poole crossed West End Avenue, going in the direction of Mason's Cafeteria. "Huh," he commented without looking around at the woman. "Sure looks like a strange one all right."

The woman smiled, then went on with her own version. "Son of one of ow-ah so-called doctors of divinity," she said. "Over at Vand-a-bilt School uh Divinity. Name of Bert Poole. The boy. And he's slightly off. Slightly *buggo*. Says Mayor Horn has sold out his people, now isn't that the most ridiculous . . . Sold out to whom, I'd like to know? . . ."

Thomas Berryman shrugged his shoulders. He started to walk off with *The Dream* and a few schedules rolled up in his hand.

"Oh, I thank you for these," he smiled and waved back like Tom the Baker. "Very good work here. Wish you lots of luck, too."

Claude, Texas, June 29, 30

Retired circuit judge Tom Berryman's house is twenty-one ramshackle rooms on the road to Amarillo, Texas.

It's a pink stucco house with green tile. Surrounded by unkempt hedgerows gleaming with large yellow roses, it sits lonely at the center of fifty thousand acres. There's a swimming pool, but it's deep in weeds, and looks more like a ruined garden than a pool.

The whole area is ugly, almost supernaturally ugly and sad.

In need of rest, however—at least a day's good rest; in need of a Mexican visa in the name of William Keresty, Thomas Berryman went to Texas. He took a Braniff jet, and then, because he'd sometimes fantasized the scene, he rented a limousine and drove home in the twenty-two foot Lincoln.

Since his 1963 stroke in Austin, old Tom Berryman had been confined to a wheelchair. Each morning, Sergeant Ames would push him out among the twisted vines and monstrous sunflowers of his garden. There, the retired Texas Ranger would talk and read, and the wasted judge would only occasionally nod or open his puffy mouth to smile or curse. More often than not he'd just think about dying in the military hospital in Austin.

When old Tom Berryman got especially tired, his head would hang back as if he was finally dead. So it was that Young Tom popped in on him completely out of the blue (that blue being the high Texas sky). Young Tom was carrying about thirty shiny magazines that the old man knew must be for him.

As Berryman came up from the garages, he was struck with the arresting thought that his father was a stone on wheels; a two-wheeled boulder; a rolling tombstone. The old man was situated in the garden, and Sergeant Ames was sporadically putting a Lucky Strike down into his mouth.

Berryman passed beside a bawling cow in the garden. Slapped at its big swinging tail. Wondered if Ames ever struck out at his father. Struck out at the very idea of the old judge reduced to such wreckage.

Judge Berryman brightened immediately as his son appeared in an upside-down scene of pear trees and sunflowers and sky. Ames was so excited he spilled lemonade on his trousers.

"Lo Thomas," his father managed with great effort. But he was up at attention, his hands were fluttering, and he was smiling. For some reason, decoration perhaps, Sergeant Ames had allowed a Wild Bill Hickok mustache to grow around his father's lip. It was stiff and dead-looking.

"I brought the *Times* and these books for Bob to read to you," Berryman spoke very slowly.

Then he dipped down and hugged the old man, let him feel the strength and life in his arms. The judge's shirt smelled punky, like babies' clothes.

Young Tom rose and fiddled around with the paper. "So what do you think of Johnny Connally?" He avoided his father's eyes.

"Boy's doing al-right, Tom." The judge grinned wider and wider, even pausing in the slow speech. "Al-right for himself, I'd say."

Neglected for the moment, the old ranger had poured everyone iced-tea glasses of lemonade. "Hey Tom, watch this," he said with a boy's grin. And to prove that he was fit as ever (Berryman later guessed), the old man swooped up a garden toad and ate it.

After he and Sergeant Ames had spoon-fed his father an imprudent but satisfying dinner of frijoles and red peppers, and after the old man had won a bid for some B & B before bed, Berryman took the limousine out on Ranch Road 3.

Mesmerized behind the wheel, he just let the unmended

fences, and the loose ponies and cows, work on his mind. He let the mesquite and prickly pear, and the pearl-white pools of alkaline water do their dirty work.

Inside the dust bowl of a little desert valley, Thomas Berryman eased down barefoot on the Lincoln's accelerator. Warm air rushed in through all the windows. Texarkana roadmaps whipped around the back windowsill. The striped red line of the speedometer moved over 100 and a safety device buzzed. The radio blared. Merle Haggard, then Tammy Wynette, then Ferlin Husky, all three plaintive and usual. But the limousine, with its speedometer marked for 120, would run no faster than 101.

Driving that way, stuck at 101, Berryman remembered being stuck at 84 in a black Ford pickup. Running through irrigation ditches. Running over bushes head-on. Missing a cow, and soft, instant death. Killing a chicken.

He remembered Ben Toy drinking warm beer and singing corny Mexican love songs. And coyote balls hanging from the Ford's rearview mirror. And snuggling up with girlfriends and watching bullbats swoop over sad shallow ponds.

Country living was a turned crock of shit, he thought.

Over a bumpy half-mile stretch, he pulled the big car off the dirt road. He got out and went around to the trunk for his rifle. He'd wrapped it in a horse blanket. It, too, smelled of dung.

He set the gun on the car roof, then sat on the fender fishing shells out of his pockets. These too he set on the roof. He slowly loaded the rifle as a peach-colored sun half-blinded him and made him think of sunstroke. The word, "sunstroke."

Berryman put the rifle under his chin, and looked at the desert through its crystal-clear sight.

There were telephone poles that were connected to nothing. With functionless blue-green cups up and down their sides. There was an ancient highway BUMP sign. Its black lettering stretched high on rusted gold.

There was a puny rabbit peeking out of a hole in the ground. And a bird with a song like electricity. Berryman could see bacteria squirming in the hot air.

He squeezed the trigger. Lightly, like a piano player.

The slender rifle barked. Jerked to the right. The BUMP sign was left intact.

Berryman carefully squeezed again. Nothing.

He took more time. Barely touching the trigger. Knowing *he had* the crotch of the *M*. Missing everything.

Berryman fired and missed. Fired and missed. He began to perspire. His arms and eyes weren't making sense together. He stopped everything.

He set the rifle against the car for a moment and collected his thoughts. It was his style. Automatic.

He calmly unscrewed the rifle's sight with his penknife. He fired a single shot without the sight. Gold metal disappeared and the BUMP sign burst open through its back.

Berryman continued until he had shot the sign away. Made it nothing. Then he drove on.

He didn't recognize the outskirts of Amarillo. There were hundreds of quick-food stops. Supermarkets with corny names. Drive-ins showing quadruple beaver movie features.

He stopped at one of the many taco places. He had a beer, and then he called an old girlfriend named Bobbie Sue Gary, now Bobbie Sue Pederson.

Sitting on the orange tile floor outside the phone booth, Thomas Berryman talked to the girl about old times. He gulped sweat-cold Pearl tallboys. Smoked a half a pack of Picayunes. Ate a taco that was tasty as a fist.

"My husband's a night shift supervisor for Shell Oil," Bobbie Sue said.

"There are airplanes and bats flying all over this desert." Berryman reported on the scene out the Taco Palace window.

"Well, I have three children now. And one in the hopper," Bobbie Sue reported.

"Well, I don't give a flying fuck," Berryman said. "I want you to get into a party dress. We're going to party."

"Tom," she complained in a lighthearted, giggling voice. "You're just trying to get into my panties all over again. I'm married now. No more hotsy-totsies for Bobbie. I have my responsibilities now."

"Oh, come on Bobbie." Thomas Berryman was laughing hard, "Don't you want to get into my pants?"

That said, he told her he was on his way.

Bobbie Sue Gary Pederson had grown slightly rat-faced over the years. The nipples of her breasts were dark brown and showing through her blouse. They looked unattractive.

On account of all this he took her to the dark cocktail lounge at the 7-10 Bowling Alleys. But he was pleased with her looks. Really.

Bobbie Sue wore a red A-line skirt umbrellaed out over seamed stockings. She wore black pumps with blue ribbons over her toes. She drank Singapore Slings, and they both ate the special chicken-fried steaks.

Thomas Berryman got high on Bobbie Sue.

"What's it like," he asked, "kissing old Tommy Pederson? Just tell me that one thing. I'll go away from here content. I'll sing in that jet back to New York City."

She was patting his leg and saying, "Now, now, now." It was just like he'd never gone away and they were still high school sweethearts.

"Don't give me that now, now, now stuff. C'mon, babe."

"It's like kissin . . . Noooo . . ."

"C'mon, babe. 'Fess up, Rev'ren Thomas is here . . ."

"Like a rug on a floor. Kissin it."

"Ooh, Bobbie Sue!" Berryman howled with delight.

"That's terrible, babe." He was laughing, and talking southern, and she thought he was hilarious.

A white moon rode the dark Texas skies as they forni- cated in the big cushy Lincoln.

Sergeant Ames found him asleep in the rocker beside his father's bed. It was morning. The judge's thing was lying out of his pajamas, large as a king post.

As he revived the judge, Sergeant Ames told Young Tom an old story about falling asleep on a cattle drive. Waking and finding he was being circumcised.

Old Tom Berryman just lay on the bed and looked at the paperback on the floor near the rocker. It was *Jiminy*. After some puckering and smacking his lips, he asked his son if he was reading about Jimmie Horn.

"Well, yes I am," Berryman said.

"Well, good for you then." The old man struggled with each word. "He seems . . . He seems . . . like a hell of a good nigger."

Berryman spent the morning back in Amarillo, ar- ranging for the visa in the name of Keresty. His supplier was an egotistical Mexican artiste who hand-lettered the document himself. For his morning's drawing he earned three hundred dollars.

That afternoon, Berryman flew back to meet the man who was paying heavily to have Horn killed. This man was ex-Tennessee Governor Jefferson Johnboy Terrell.

Thomas Berryman was calm as a snake after its sunbath.

Nashville, October 12

This past October 12th, Columbus Day, was the kind of unexpectedly cold day that makes grown men, like me, sleep through their alarm clocks.

That morning—a flat, gray, homely one—the state had its first frost.

That afternoon, ex-Governor Jefferson Terrell was driven into downtown Nashville to face a grand jury on the charge that he had paid over one hundred thousand dollars to accomplish the murder of James Horn the previous July.

Terrell's car, a somber, black, 1969 Fleetwood, was chauffeured by a soldiery-looking man with short sandy hair brushed back like Nixon's Mr. Haldeman.

Terrell's new lawyer, a slick gray fox (also from Houston), was riding in the back seat with him.

The media coverage for the upcoming trial had by this time risen above the noise level of Procter and Gamble's newest soap detergent commercials.

People would hear about the trial on the radio coming home from work; then find it staring up at them from the newspaper on their front porch; then get hit with it on both the local and network TV news programs.

People from the hills were already planning weekends around a Friday at the trial and a Saturday trip to Opryland.

• • •

Over three thousand of them greeted Terrell at the courthouse on the twelfth.

Johnboy struggled up out of the Cadillac, revealing patent leather loafers, then a gray banker's suit, then a pasty, death-mask face.

Not that much had changed about Terrell's general demeanor though.

He *held* one of his familiar dollar cigars instead of smoking it. But otherwise, it was the way he'd been around the capitol for all the years I'd ever seen him there.

He shook a few hands and gave a proper politician's wave all around. *Yes his health was just fine*, he answered a query from some well-wisher in a checkered bird-dog hat.

Then a little man in a gray raincoat got ahold of Terrell's hand and wouldn't let him go.

"Bad times," the man was heard to say a few times.

"But it's a good, strong country all the same," Johnboy told him. "Isn't it a good country we've got here, my friend?"

The eyes of the man in the raincoat blinked on and off. Then he let go of Terrell's hand.

Johnboy then bulled his way up the forty-three courthouse stairs and disappeared inside without once looking back.

"He'd make a fine corpse," Lewis Rosten muttered from somewhere behind me. "Mr. Dickens, in his neat mystery *Martin Chuzzlewit*."

During the secretive grand jury proceedings, the newspapermen and TV guys sat around the second floor of the courthouse drinking free Folger's coffee.

Occasionally we'd get official word that *nothing* was happening. Some Nashville policeman had the job of coming in to tell us that nothing was happening.

His one big news break was the information that ex-Governor Terrell had taken some pills from a little black snap case just before he went in to meet with the grand jury.

A long-haired northern reporter stood up and said with a straight face, "Sergeant, could you give us anything on the *color* of the pills?"

That was the big laugh of the morning. In fact, that *was* the morning.

Just after lunch, though, we finally got a little surprise.

A Tom Wolfe-ish young man (the *new* Tom Wolfe) walked into the press room to make an important announcement for Mr. Terrell.

He was a little dandy, in a white suit and polka-dot bow tie. Yale, without any doubt. Word went out that he was Terrell's own son.

"Contrary to the suspicions of many of you here," he read from a small brown pad, "my father is not planning to sneak out a back door to a second Cadillac after these proceedings." The petulant young man looked up at us as though he'd really stung it to us. "Following the grand jury session," he continued without aid of his pad, "Mr. Terrell will entertain questions from the press outside." With that, Terrell's son stalked out of the room.

Well, you've heard the speech Terrell gave several times over these past few sad years in America.

It's the one that never fails to bug your eyes and put a ringing in your ears. It's the same speech that proved that Nixon, and Mitchell, and Connally, and all the others, despised us to the point of ridiculing us to our faces.

Standing up on the white courthouse steps, Terrell seemed overly casual to me. Confident. Thoroughly despicable.

And in the sincerest voice I could remember hearing out of him, in a voice choking with moral outrage, he said that he "welcomed the chance to prove his innocence once and for all, before a judicial system that he for one still believed in."

Some people booed loudly; more people cheered.

He went on to say how he was confident that "the courts will vindicate me." And he said, "I swear to you before my Lord and Savior, that I have done nothing wrong, and nothing to be ashamed of."

It was as strange and scary then as it was the first time I heard a grown adult serve up that kind of tripe to a group of other adults.

An even more frightening thing was in store for me that afternoon.

I'd gone down near the Fleetwood to observe the crowd up close. I was standing with a long-haired *Citizen-Reporter* photographer putting it all down on film.

To a man the people down by the Cadillac had that sick, hurt look I've never seen so much as at the Bible Belt showings of a movie called *Marjoe*. *Marjoe* is a documentary about a young, very well loved evangelist who openly admits how he's been lying to and defrauding the people of the South. I want to tell you that the people around here cried after seeing that film. They are basically trusting, and they can't comprehend deceit at that high a level.

At any rate, I was busy watching this fussed-up crowd, and I never saw Terrell until he was practically on top of me. In fact, I only saw him because the photographer started snapping away like a madman.

Johnboy never stepped one foot out of his chosen path, but he raised a stubby index finger and pointed at me from about ten feet or so away.

He looked at me with all the pride and Son-of-God feelings power can give a weak man. He looked and pointed, and all he said was "You."

I've got the photograph to prove that, too. It's hanging safe and sound, blown up into proportion over my fireplace up here in Poland County.

Standing in front of the Tennessee state courthouse that day, October 12, I took the wild guess that Terrell would never be tried and convicted. That turned out to be right.

Nashville, June 30

A wasted American dreamer, Jefferson Terrell is 99% fat now. He has greasy, cardboard-colored hair slickly parted down the middle, but ducktailing in back. He constantly smells of tobacco and mash whiskey, and since he's developed high blood pressure his plump face is tomato red. Johnboy also has a big, lazy accent. He pronounces words like pleasure, "play-sure."

But there is a smoldering brain in the wreck of Terrell's body, and he is the man who finally got Thomas Berryman.

• • •

They met to exchange money in a top-floor suite in the old Walter Scott Hotel near the Old Opry Building and Tootsie's Orchard Lounge. Berryman showed up late. He wore a yellow rubber terrorist's mask for the meeting.

Still, an open Amana freezer couldn't have dominated the tacky hotel sitting room any more than Johnboy. The man had presence; he'd always had it.

He'd ordered Beam's Pin, and he was lounging over a squash-yellow davenport, drinking the overrated whiskey without ice. He told Berryman that he looked like a State Farm Insurance agent. His clothes did. Terrell said nothing about the mask, though it clearly had surprised him.

Trapped inside the stuffy room, Berryman wanted to be back outdoors. Where it was breezy and sunny and quiet. More than that, he wanted to be done with this job, and with the *Souf*.

"You may consider it foolhardy that I've chosen to meet with you myself," Johnboy said. "Well, I agree. It is foolish. But it's the way I've always done things. I am a southerner, an empiricist. I wanted to talk to you. To evaluate you. To see you, I had hoped."

Thomas Berryman nodded. He was catching sunstreaks in the brass minor behind Terrell's head. He was remembering Oona Quinn coming out of the Atlantic Ocean like the girl in the famous airline commercial.

"Now you stop me if I'm not making sense . . ."

"You're doing fine," Berryman spoke through the rubber mask.

Terrell slowly sipped his bourbon. He examined Berryman like a rich man undecided about a new stud horse. "I was curious about the kind of man you are. I was damn curious after that row with poor Wynn."

Berryman found himself smiling at the fat man's manner. "And what do you think now?"

"Why, I find you a complete surprise," Terrell laughed. "You're so smart, you see." He laughed again. "I even begin to wonder why you bother with this sad business."

"Sometimes I wonder, too," Berryman said. "But I guess I'm wondering more about the rest of my money right now. In fact, I'm beginning to worry. I thought you understood that I was to be paid before I do any work. I may be smart, but I'm also very expensive."

Terrell was a little surprised. "You haven't begun?"

"I've done a few little things. Horn is a difficult target given your requirements. I'm ready to begin."

"Money then." The fat man patted his suitjacket. "Right here. Right over the ole ticker. Thomas Berryman," he kept repeating the name. "I think I expected much more of a lightweight. A lightweight personality, that is. I believe I oversimplified."

Berryman replied in a soft, southern gentleman's voice that he borrowed from his father.

"I am a lightweight," he leveled Johnboy. "I have bad emotional reflexes. I'm basically very lazy. Very materialistic. I want to get away from it all. Fast. Live the good life, you know."

Johnboy's head bobbed and his chest heaved a little. He was slightly amused. "Sounds familiar enough." He reached inside his suitjacket.

He took out a brown packet bound in ordinary elastic bands. The package was about three inches thick. "All in all, one hundred thousand to the good life," he said rather solemnly.

He sat and studied Berryman as he opened the money and flipped through the crisp bills. He appreciated Berryman's attention to detail. Berryman looked the part of a southern businessman. Right down to the matching tie clasp, cufflinks, belt buckle; to the gray rayon socks with red clocks on the sides.

"I do admire your inventiveness, Berryman. You are no hunter. If you live long enough, I'm sure you'll get everything that you want."

Berryman finished his counting, then tucked the money in his suitjacket. He stood up over the davenport, moved in front of a confused oil painting of the Scopes trial, and Terrell got up with him.

"I may be using a gun this time," Berryman said. "I want lots of confusion. Confusion is the key. It will look very good for the papers. It will probably happen on the Fourth of July. Probably."

Berryman was wearing light yellow driving gloves and he extended one hand to Terrell. "I don't mean to be rude," he continued to speak softly, "but I really shouldn't spend any more time here. It's stupid of me to be here at all."

Johnboy touched the glove lightly, more exploring than shaking hands. He stared into the mask's eyeholes for a full ten seconds. "So damn smart," he said once again.

Berryman nodded and smiled slightly. "If I'm followed out of here," he said, "the deal is off. You mustn't interfere."

• • •

Around that same time in the early evening, Jimmie Horn's hazel-brown eyes drifted down from melodramatic paintings of Jesus posed in front of various wooden doors and gates . . . to autographed photographs of Jesse Jackson, Julian Bond, Langston Hughes . . . to a collection of every black person Norman Rockwell had ever drawn.

Then the one person he was consistently unable to fool or inveigle, a large-breasted seventy-one-year-old schoolteacher, walked into the parlor where he was sitting. She carried bubbling tonic water with lime, and warm sugar and lemon cakes. She was Etta Raide Horn, his mother.

"Should of taught summer school again." She sat in a creaky rocker currently painted green. "Already missin those little stinkers, Jiminy."

Horn shook his head. "You should get out of that school altogether is what you *should*. He should get out of the grocery, too."

"And you should go back into law practice," Mrs. Horn said.

Her son laughed. "So there."

"So there to yourself." She maintained a straight face that only hinted at laughter. "By way, Mr. Mayor, how's your campaign going?"

"It's going very well, I think." Horn took a sugar cake, closed his eyes, slowly let his teeth cut through it.

"I see," Etta Horn nodded. "I see."

She sipped her cool drink, watching her son over the rim.

"I've been talking to a few people about it. Politics," she clarified. "I've been sitting down at the store musing about it. Listening to quite a few people talk too."

Jimmie Horn looked over her head at Julian Bond's photo. He wondered what Bond's folks were like. "So what's on your mind?" he asked his mother.

"Oh, nothing. Nothing." The old woman revealed where her son might have picked up his great innocent postures. "We did visit your Aunt Fay down at Clarksville last week though."

"Uh-huh," Horn shook his head.

"Farming niggers down there don't know Jimmie Horn from Harry the Hootowl," she grinned. "White folks down there know you, but they don't approve of you."

"You're beating around the bush, darlin'. You've got me flushed out. Talk straight."

"Well," Etta Horn sighed, "it just seems to me . . . you've got to meet with these people. You've got to reach out, and shake their hands, and tell'm who you are. Got to have people saying—'Hey now, guess who I saw down the feed store today. That young Jimmie Horn runnin' for United States Senator. He looked me right in my eye, said he'd be the finest, hardest-working senator Tennessee has ever had.'

"Why I heard of a man somewhere," Etta Horn went on, "Michigan, Ohio? . . . he won senator just by walking across the state meetin' people face to face."

"Black fella?" Jimmie Horn smiled.

"Don't get smart. Don't get wise . . . People like a hardworker, black, white, or otherwise. Especially these days. All these bums around."

"All right." Jimmie Horn rubbed his hands together for action. "All right. You walking with me?"

The old woman jutted out her chin. "I'll walk," she said. "Far as my legs carry me."

"Will your husband walk?"

"He hates it like the plague of Egypt—politics—but he'll be there too."

Horn sat back in his chair. He bit off another mouthful of cake. "Love these things," he smiled.

Etta Horn just sat quietly rocking in her green chair. She rocked and nodded and winked one time. She looked like a woman capable of plotting a President up from his cradle.

"You're sneaky as you ever were," she finally said with the familiar straight face.

"You're not so bad yourself."

Before Jimmie Horn left that evening, his father wandered in from the grocery.

He was Marblehead Horn, squarely built, forever in farmer's overalls and a gray felt hat. He looked like a black Nikita Khrushchev.

"Daddy, we've got you out campaigning with Jimmie," Etta Horn told him as a greeting.

"The hell you do." Marblehead plopped down in his easy chair. "Shit on that."

"We're going to walk clear across Tennessee. Just like that man in Ohio."

Horn's father punched the TV remote control. An ancient Zenith flared in the corner of the living room. "The hell I am," he called back to her.

But he would. He always had, and he would. The old man was a sure thing. Just as sure as the fact that his Little Hill Grocery opened at six, closed at nine-thirty, took credit for "anything people eat, and nothing else."

Jimmie Horn went home that night with warm feelings

coursing through his body. This time a black Galaxie joined the green Polara that always followed him.

• • •

At 11 P.M., a pale blue Lincoln Continental shut off in the porte cochere of one of the dark, fat plantation estates in Nashville's Belle Meade section.

Terrell climbed heavily out of the car, paused like a thoughtful animal in the porch light, then disappeared into his house.

Bright lights flashed on in several rooms on the ground floor level. They mapped his route through the big house.

The final light was the desk lamp in Terrell's study.

Terrell sat down in a worn easy chair. He slid off his black patent leather loafers, loosened his belt, thought about this Thomas Berryman character for a moment. He thought about the lawyer Harley John Wynn too. About his murder somewhere up in New York.

Then he made a phone call to New Orleans.

The man Terrell spoke to in Louisiana had a fast, nearly unintelligible drawl. "This Berryman the one who does the drownings and heart attacks?" he wanted to know. "This *Thomas* Berryman you yappin' about, Mister Terrell?"

"Thomas Berryman," Johnboy said. "But I believe he'll be using a gun this time. That's the impression I got. I had a nice little talk with the man. Southern boy, you know."

During the next few minutes the details of a contract on Thomas Berryman were arranged. A mob killer would probably be used. He was to be paid in full regardless of what happened to Jimmie Horn.

"Your nigger is Thomas Berryman's responsibility," the New Orleans man made very clear. "He's the hot-shit. My man's fee will be ten. He's light. He's mob."

"By the way, Mr. Terrell," the New Orleans man quipped before he hung up, "this is turning into a real public service number for you, isn't it."

After Terrell hung up, the New Orleans man called first New York, then Philadelphia. The name Joseph Cubbah was brought up during the Philadelphia call.

Nashville, July 1

An attempt on Horn would have been made on Sunday night. An attempt was made.

At about seven-thirty, Santo Massimino was studying ten Jimmie Horns on videotape monitors, and he was liking all of them.

The young media flash was stalking Tennessee in a WWII flight jacket and ice-cream-store pants. He was a N.Y. hippie, but a serious, wooden-faced one. He was also one of America's finest salesmen. Right up there with Arthur Godfrey. Massimino's secret was to talk fast, make as little *real* sense as possible, and give people absolutely no chance to consider what he was saying.

Jimmie Horn has a news commentator's face, Massimino was thinking to himself. It was a good TV face. It filled up the gray screen in a nice way and made you feel pretty good about politics. About life in general. That was the way Horn would be merchandised.

Massimino walked away from the monitor Horns, and called out in the direction of the real McCoy. "No way, Thirsty," he called. "Take the mike off his tie. We'll go with the offstage mike."

Jimmie Horn was being prepared for a half-hour TV broadcast at eight.

Thurston Frey, a long-haired station hand, finished nailing down an apple-red carpet around Horn's armchair. Then he gingerly picked the microphone off the mayor's silk tie.

Meanwhile, Horn's appointments secretary was reading him a riot-act fact sheet by way of prepping him for the TV show.

Off to one side, Horn's best friend, Jap Quarry, sipped Navy coffee on a couch used on the "Noon" local TV show. Ten-year-old Keesha Horn was with him. Little boys were already taking after-school jobs to raise money to take pretty Keesha to movies like *Superfly* and *Claudine*. (Except that lately she'd had to go to movies, and even to school, with a policeman.)

Quarry suddenly roared out cruel laughter. The welfare worker stomped over to Jimmie Horn on big orange work boots. He presented the mayor with the styrofoam coffee cup he'd just drained. He shook his head sadly. ELECT HORN SENATOR was printed on the cup's inside bottom.

"Such bullshit, man," Jap Quarry said. "Pure, pure, 100% pure, bullshit, Jim."

"Television and radio commercials," the appointments secretary read on from the fact sheet, "are just extensions of the whistle stop."

"One hundred percent pure, Jim. How much do you want it?"

A makeup man put a touch of light pancake on the mayor's chin. Then he wiped it off.

Santo Massimino stood jabbing a rich ward chairman named Heck Worth in the cowboy shirt. "I want you to personally take full responsibility for the busing of the Nashville Technical and the Nashville Pearl High School marching bands," he said to this man who had made a million dollars out of mere apple cider.

A sound man crept up alongside the makeup man and started to whisper to the mayor. "I need a level on you, Mayor."

"I cannot stand this confusion and noise," the mayor said to him.

"Thank you."

Massimino entertained a woman caller on the station telephone line. She was Betsy Ribbin calling from Clarksville, Tennessee. She was fifty-seven years old, married, with six grown-up children. She was undecided about Mayor Horn, but she welcomed the opportunity to question him on the special TV program.

Massimino had already decided to open the show with this sweet-voiced woman.

On the other side of a gold, sequined curtain, a small live audience was listening to the mc of the "Noon" television show. He was warming them up for the broadcast, not so much telling funny stories, as telling stories funny. Sometimes he'd disappear behind the curtain and two guitars and a drum would play songs like "The beer that made Milwaukee famous, made a loser out of me." Everybody liked that.

Thomas Berryman sat near the rear in the far left aisle.

He tapped his shoes to the music, laughed at the country corn, and made friendseeking small talk with the people around him.

Berryman also watched the audience for the appearance of the long-haired man. One nicely dressed boy of about twelve wore a button, *Where Are You Lee Harvey Oswald, Now That We Need You?*

Horn came on without fanfare. He was wearing a light gray suit. A light blue shirt. A dark blue tie. His stomach was queasy, as if he'd stayed up all night.

Sitting down by the interview phone, Horn remembered a time in his freshman year in the state legislature. He had been talking through his hat, practicing his public speaking more or less, and then he'd noticed that Estes

Kefauver was watching him from the balcony. After the session, Kefauver had approached him in the hallway. "Young man," he'd said in the most low-key manner, "you are one of the finest public speakers I have ever had the privilege of watching. In the future, try not to talk, when you don't have anything to say."

The telephone rang. Jimmie Horn picked it up in a businesslike way.

"Helloo. Helloo. Is this really Mayor Horn?" Betsy Ribbin asked in her sweet drawl.

"It sure is," Jimmie Horn smiled at the lens of the TV camera. "Now who is this?"

Betsy Ribbin gave her name and city, and then she brought up the subject she'd just been talking about with Santo Massimino. The subject was law and order.

"Why I just used to talk with anyone who was in need of help or even a little smile," she said by way of explaining the current situation in Clarksville, Tennessee. "I used to start up a conversation with anyone," she said. "But now, many of my friends have been robbed and hit over the head. I am afraid of people now . . . Moral statistics," she concluded, "are very low in Clarksville, Tennessee."

"When you hear the two beeps," Santo Massimino instructed a caller who identified himself as a divinity student, "take a beat, count to three, and then tell Jimmie your name and hometown. OK?"

"Er, um, my name and my hometown," Bert Poole said.

• • •

His phone beeped twice, he counted three and he took a deep breath.

"Er, Mister Horn?" he said.

"Yes, it is," Jimmie Horn nodded to the Conrac camera. "Who is this?"

"Um, um," Poole said.

"Before you start. Could you just tell us who you are," Jimmie Horn asked. "Who you are, and where you're from?"

"My name uh, doesn't matter."

"We just like each caller to identify himself. It just makes it a little easier for me."

"You already know me, sort of. Anyway, it's Bert, OK. What's important, um, um, er um, is that I tell you why I'm going to kill you."

Santo Massimino waved his arms over his head and screamed something that no one understood or remembered later on. The phone call was cut off in the studio.

A roar, a roar or a groan, went up from the live audience.

The television audience heard a prearranged chorus of "Yesterday." It was the music used on the "Noon" show. There was a ten-second delay on broadcast, so they never heard Poole.

Horn was back on with a Pi Delta from the University of Tennessee.

• • •

When the half-hour show ended, Massimino quickly detoured Horn through a back room full of videotape machines.

They walked through a room full of coughing generators. Then down a light flight of gray stairs.

"You don't have to run," Horn said.

Massimino didn't answer. He was frightened.

The stairs led to a small, private parking lot. It was drizzling outside, and quite muggy.

A crowd of fifteen to twenty people had already gathered for a close-up look at Horn. In his rain-spattered pea-green suit, Thomas Berryman was among them.

Less than fifteen yards away his Ford was throwing smoke in the night like a factory. It was pointed out toward the state highway. This was a fairly dark country road. It went nowhere—north; and toward a maze of drive-ins and gas stations—south.

The crowd was predominately children. There were some women. And two hillbilly fathers.

Horn's chauffeur, a short, bulldog black, stepped out of the Cadillac. It too was blowing smoke.

Berryman tightened his grip on a four-inch .38. He glanced back to make sure his car was still clear to the road. He looked around for police or more adults. Then he pushed his way to the rear fins of the Cadillac. Horn would have to pass right by him.

Massimino wasn't letting the mayor shake any hands. He had him tightly by the elbow. He was marching him straight for the Cadillac.

Jimmie Horn was using his finger to windshield-wipe his dark glasses. Walking together, he and Massimino looked like businessmen on a hurried lunch hour.

Jap Quarry suddenly ran into the rain out the back door. He corraled Horn in a big friendly arm. He laughed and shook hands on the run, and quickly had Horn inside the car.

Berryman backed away. He stood nearby and clapped as the gray Cadillac slowly pulled out of the lot.

As Jap Quarry closed the electric back window, and Horn opened it a crack, Berryman was already conjecturing that the next time might be a little harder. At any rate, the Horn number had begun.

• • •

Life was understated inside the big gray El Dorado. The windshield wipers *swished* gently, never *thunked*. The air conditioner hummed pleasantly, like the machines some people use as sleep aids. The soft leather seats never creaked, just inhaled, exhaled.

No one in the car was talking and Santo Massimino nervously switched on the radio.

The song was "Stand by Your Man," and it seemed ridiculous to be playing Tammy Wynette in a car full of blackmen. For once in his life the young dissimulator was at a loss for the proper covering gesture.

He pressed the button on the radio's far left and it was the one for the station that was already playing.

Horn's little bulldog driver snorted through his nose; he switched road lanes with one hand.

"Don't touch that dii-ll," Jap Quarry put on a country and western voice in the back seat. "You don't never switch the dii-ll on Tammy, San-to"

The dog-faced driver thought that was quite funny too. Quarry reached up front and tousled Massimino's hair to let him know the joke wasn't purposely on him.

A lighter flared in the back and Massimino saw Jimmie Horn in the rearview mirror. In the brief light the mayor had seemed dazed.

"I don't think I mentioned it, Jimmie," Massimino finally came up with something to talk about, "but we worked out a deal with Luby Cadillac today. With his son."

"Myron," Horn said from his rear corner. "Myron's all right."

"Yeah, he really is. He's giving us a car until November."

Horn glanced over at Jap Quarry, then leaned forward, closer to Massimino. "No Cadillacs," he said in a soft voice, softer than usual, a dazed voice. "I feel like Willie Stark or something in a Cadillac. It embarrasses my people."

"We don't agree," Massimino said.

"Oh, OK, what *do* I feel like then, Santo?"

"That's not what I mean. We think it's a bad move."

"Why is it a bad move?" Horn asked. "Jap, now why would it be a bad move if I didn't drive around in a Cadillac?"

Massimino swiveled around in the front seat. Cars

coming up from the rear backlit his hair like an old psychedelic poster. "You want me to speak plain?" he said.

"Of course I want you to speak plain."

"All right then, we—myself, Jap Quarry, everybody down here who gives a shit about you—we all feel that you shouldn't turn down this particular Cadillac." Massimino was suddenly sounding very intelligent and convincing. "And the reason we feel that way is that this Cadillac is coming in special from Detroit. It has bullet-proof glass in all the windows."

Nashville, October 17, 18

Nathanial Brown, Jr., twenty-three, a black American, an assistant cameraman with the WNET-TV affiliate in Nashville, had filmed the shooting of Jimmie Horn in grainy 16mm color—home movie quality.

Within six hours of the shooting, that washed-out clip was picked up by every major TV station in America. It was viewed with morbid fascination in more than forty other countries. Print-quality photographs were made off the film, and they appeared in newspapers as well as the national newsmagazines.

The *Citizen-Reporter* received a black and white dup of Brown's film the day of the shooting. It wasn't until I returned from the North, however, that anybody studied the footage in detail.

First one of our art men snipped out the individual frames and had them mounted on slides. Then Lewis Rosten, Reed, and myself spent the better part of two days projecting Kodak slide after slide onto a plaster wall in Reed's darkened office.

It was a curious, nauseating experience for all three of us.

Each of us took turns standing at the wall with a school-teacher's wooden pointer, moving from face to shadowy face on the black and white slides.

First we looked for Thomas Berryman. We examined every face on every frame, even sending out for super blowups of distorted or partially hidden men.

We found Berryman on none of the slides, however.

Our next step was to examine the footage of the shooting itself. Either because Nathanial Brown had to pan his camera too rapidly, or because the people around him were bumping the camera, this footage was partially blurred.

Bert Poole was visible in two short sequences just prior to the shooting. Though two minutes apart on the film, both pieces showed Poole in precisely the same pose: he was huddled against restraining ropes, both of his arms inside a khaki, army-style jacket. He seemed to be sick; possibly he was frightened, though.

The man from Philadelphia, Joe Cubbah, was shown clearly in one seven-second sequence.

But no Thomas Berryman.

• • •

Both Bert Poole and Jimmie Horn were on camera when the pistol was drawn.

The distance between them was about ten feet; the first shot seemed to strike Horn somewhere at the top of his chest. The impact of the bullet knocked him backward and Reed said a .44 would do that.

The first shot was followed by a blurry sequence in which both Horn and Poole were on camera. There were a lot of inappropriate lights and shadows here. (The sequence lasted seventy frames, or just under three seconds.)

Seconds after that (another ninety frames to look at), both Poole and Jimmie Horn had fallen and were out of the camera shot.

After studying the film for two days (Rosten and I had been looking at it for four days), our opinion was that Poole had definitely shot Horn, and that Berryman had probably been planning the shooting later—if at all that day.

Our opinion, however, was completely wrong.

Nashville, Late October

An equally bad mistake (for me at least) came in our investigation of Bert Poole.

By the end of the summer, tomes of material had already been gathered on Poole.

Poole, the educators said, had a low, but certainly not a defective intellect. Poole, the psychologists said, was under strong pressures to realize himself in some way. Poole had an ambiguous and inconsistent attitude toward Jimmie Horn. Poole had been addicted to adventure comic books as a boy. Poole had been in homosexual panic at the time of the shooting.

But Moses Reed felt that we needed more information. Life-style material. *In Cold Blood* detail. "Poole was fucked up," Reed said, "but I'm convinced that Poole wasn't simply a nut."

So I spent nearly two weeks contacting Bert Poole's relatives and his friends.

His mother and father had already refused interviews to the major magazines and other newspapers, but Lewis felt I ought to approach them anyway. He reasoned that I was the only one working under the assumption that their son might *not* be a murderer.

During one week in October I reached Mrs. Helen Poole several times on the telephone.

She was courteous and cooperative, but she always ended up telling me the same thing: "Doctor Poole is making all the decisions about Bert. But Doctor Poole isn't at home right now."

At 8 A.M., 12 noon, 7 P.M., 10 P.M.—Doctor Poole was never home.

One night, though, I decided I had to camp out at the Pooles' and find out some things for myself.

Their home was a modest split-level on Whippland Road in Nashville's Brentwood section. It was a very neat place, kept up, certainly in character for a divinity school professor.

I parked across the street from the Pooles', and I immediately got a lot of strange looks from the neighbors. One or two of them came by and gave me lectures on privacy.

Then around eleven o'clock, with me just about to go under from an overdose of AM radio, Doctor Leland Poole finally turned into his driveway.

The taillights of his Pontiac station wagon flashed red. The heavy car scraped bottom on the street's drainage ditch. Then he eased it up in front of his porch.

No lights were on outside the house, so I couldn't get a good look at Doctor Poole. The only detail I caught was that he wore eyeglasses. It was difficult connecting the man and his house with Bert Poole or the shooting of Horn.

Moments after he went inside I saw him in the living room window. He was tall, very tall, balding, still holding his briefcase. He was staring directly at my car.

I opened the car door and let him see me. Then I got out of the car and walked over the dark lawn.

At first I thought the Pooles weren't going to answer the doorbell. They hadn't turned on the porch light and I could feel water bugs crawling over my shoes.

Then a dim yellow light popped on over my head.

Mosquitoes went to it like candy. Leland Poole, still in his summer suit and tie, opened the front door.

Poole's father was slightly shorter than I am—maybe 64—but he didn't slouch. He was able to look me directly in the eyes.

"Ah ah-sume you uh re-portah." He spoke with a Deep South gentleman's accent. He then listened politely as I told him my name and my mission.

"Well, Mr. Jones," he said then, "I have read your articles."

I waited for elaboration on that but only a long pause came. It was a silent time during which Doctor Poole kept his mouth opened slightly.

"I should tell you," he eventually spoke again, "that owah lawyer, Mr. Huddlestone, owah lawyer, has asked us not to give out any interviews. Neither Helen or myself, Mr. Jones.

"It is Mr. Huddlestone's position that interviews would not be in our best interest. Nor would they be best for Bert.

"To be quite candid"—the professor took in a gasp of night air—"I uh . . . I don't believe that I could.

"To be candid . . . I uh, leave this house with my briefcase each morning. Uh, uh . . . and I kiss Helen goodbye . . . and Mr. Jones, without giving her any indication that I am going anyplace other than my office, or to the James Tate Library on the campus, I drive down to Murfreesboro, Tennessee. I sit around a farmhouse my father left me a few years back."

Doctor Poole then began to cry. His crying made no

sound. He neither wiped away the tears, nor tried to shut me outside.

"I just clockwatch," he said.

Nashville, July 2

The morning sun was on his dark glasses and as he moved his head from side to side the sun danced across both black frames.

Berryman slowed his car across from a small pink house on a north-numbered street in East Nashville. It was where he'd followed Bert Poole the night they'd been together in the Horn storefront. He let the car roll on, slowing cracking twigs and branches. He stopped it at the end of the street, where there is no more curb, just crabgrass.

This is a black neighborhood bordering on Fisk University ground; it's a shabby colony, chartered and owned by the First National Bank. On one corner, there is a Marlboro cigarette poster. It's backlit so that the cowboy and his horse appear black.

Thomas Berryman walked past a wooden shack laundry that reported how they harlemize clothes.

He passed a stripped Imperial, its broken windshield caked with dead insects. A broken refrigerator was strapped into its open trunk.

A lot of small children and old people and what the

children call "nigger dogs" are usually outdoors in the early morning here. That was how it was the morning Berryman came to find out what Bert Poole had on his mind.

The screen kitchen door to the pink shotgun house was in a littered alley. The door was warped, wormy wood, and it didn't quite close. It was locked by a hook.

An old air conditioner on the attic floor threw off water like an ice cube. The cold drops splashed down on Berryman's crew cut.

He rapped on the door three or four times and called out Bert Poole's name in a loud, clear voice. Then, when there was no answer, he pulled the hook out of the rotting door frame and walked inside to investigate for himself.

The back shed held the odor of a cellar full of bad apples. It got worse as Berryman passed into the kitchen. It was as if a horse was dead somewhere. Maybe mice behind the stove, Berryman thought.

There was no one in the apartment. In fact, there was hardly anything there. There were unpaid bills in the kitchen: Southern Bell; Electric; Cain-Sloan Department Stores. Cain-Sloan was threatening to repossess furniture from Poole.

A blackseated toilet was clogged, and the bathroom smelled like an outhouse.

A brownstained, blue-striped mattress was the main living room furniture. That and a chintzy brown vinyl recliner stood out in the room. One tall lamp with a picture of Martin Luther King safety-pinned to its shade was standing next to the front door.

There were looseleaf papers scattered all over the floor, and there was a leather traveling bag, the kind of expensive carryall that athletes bring to basketball games.

Berryman made himself comfortable against the wall. He sat on the gritty mattress, and held the leather bag in his lap.

It was filled with balled striped shirts and Ivy League–style ties; there were some boxer shorts and crusty socks. There was a stenciled T-shirt that said UNCLE BERT LOVES YOU. At the bottom of the bag, folded in a pair of chinos, he found a long .44 magnum pistol. Berryman set it out on the mattress.

As he waited for Poole, he read what had been written on some of the looseleaf papers.

One neatly handwritten page started:

My name is Bertram Poole. I was born in Memphis in 1948. My parents are Southern Baptist. Very good Xtians. Very good people . . .

Other papers were litanies of sentimental observations about different types of Americans. There were also passages about life in what Poole called the South of America.

One curious juxtaposition read:

My dad is a professor at Vanderbilt University. Once, he sent me to Baylor University. I was really too slow to keep up with the fast, mathematical people there. I think Dad pulled strings to get me accepted. He didn't want me to miss out on my puberty rites.

In 1966 Time *magazine named me Man of the Year. I was the "25 and under generation."*

Another page started:

I would not like to die of loneliness. I think people may have done that. But no thank you.

Sometimes, I feel I am unconnected with the world. I've either dreamed or read of people bumping into other people in crowds. To make certain they were connected. I've never actually done this. But I've thought about it enough times.

Berryman read the next paper several times.

I am obsessed with the idea of killing an important man.

I am also preoccupied with getting even with Mayor Horn. He turns out to be another heartless thug. People deserve better than that phony. That carbon copy.

He has life by the tail. People by the tail, too.

I talked to Dad about obsession. Not about specifics of course, just in general.

He says that all great men are, what you might call, obsessed. He doesn't say that I'm a great man. He tells me not to worry about it.

We went to the Divinity School cafeteria one time and ate with a very famous man in the economics department. "Yes, young Bert," he said to me, "I am very obsessed with statistics."

If Poole had come back while Berryman was sitting there reading, Berryman thought that he probably would have killed him. He'd come to the apartment to learn if the crazy-looking hippie was dangerous; now he felt that he was.

He considered shooting the saccharine maniac with his own .44 magnum.

But Poole didn't come back, and as Thomas Berryman sat reading and smoking at his leisure, he started to make more considered plans for the young southerner. Far from being an unexpected liability, he began to feel that Poole might be very useful, a godsend.

White Geese, July 2

The famous Chub L. Moss and Sons; Gunsmiths, is a gray gas station and red barn in White Geese, Kentucky. Moss specializes in legal fireworks, and also in tools for the extermination of black males. Berryman took the two-lane blacktop up to White Geese after he left Poole's apartment.

The fireworks store was full of hangdog hillbillies. Human clown faces. It took Berryman a good half hour to get to see Chub Moss, Jr.

He found the man extraordinary to look at. Moss had been shot through his head as a teenager and his eyes wandered around like pinballs.

"So how you?" He greeted Berryman with the upraised hand of a court clerk. "Bet you lookin for some Foaff of Ju-ly fah-works." He swung his hand down toward crates of bombs and hanging strips of red poppers. "Feast your eyes, stranger."

Thomas Berryman was into playacting again. He looked at his shoetips and grinned like a boy come in to buy his first Trojan. "Also lookin for a gun, Mister Moss."

Moss Jr. exposed several blackened teeth in an unhappy smile. He lowered his voice. "Wah you lookin in the exact right place mah fren. Jes keep at little cigar to you'sef. Get you face blow out yo asshole if you don't."

Moss turned on his heels and led the way to a smaller room to one side of the main fireworks emporium. Only a few men had ventured into the smaller room. It was filled with rifles and revolvers. Every kind of rifle from a Winchester .22 for rat exterminating to an M-16 smuggled out of Fort Campbell.

Moss held up one of the M-16s. "This here is more of a *weapon*, sportsman. Course? . . . " He sighted the long rifle at two young women gassing up a VW out front. His eyes flew around behind the barrel like stirred bats.

"Dreamin' of nook," Moss said, "shooting the gook." He clicked the trigger and simulated a blunderbuss recoil.

He google-eyed Berryman's sunglasses. "Hope you not thinkin a huntin rabbit?"

Berryman hooted. "Not going to eat'm if I do."

"You sure as hell ain't. No way."

Moss Jr. tried to sell Berryman a Colt .38 with an ankle holster. He tried several different M-12s and M-16s. Some twenty-two-caliber dum-dums. A hand-made Creek Indian blanket.

Berryman hemmed and hawed, toed the wooden floor like a skittish colt, finally picked up one of the Smith & Wesson pistols. A .44 magnum like Bert Poole's. Plus a silencer.

He signed for it American Express: care of Mr. Brewster Greene of Louisville.

As he bagged the gun, silencer and ammunition, one of Moss Jr.'s eyes disappeared into his forehead. In his mind he was participating. "Hey, whachu goan do with all this fahpow?"

Berryman held an Indian blanket up to a hanging Coleman lamp. "Targetshoot," he said. "Kill beer cans and watermelons."

Moss's eye returned. "You know that .44 was developed for huntin," he said.

"I know that."

"All right then. All right," Moss grinned. He handed over the gun. "You will be careful a your nigger weenies near my cherry bombs. On your way out, stranger."

Philadelphia, July 2

It was on that same day, July 2nd, that the final piece was told about the puzzle.

St. Joseph's Place is a well-kept secret in the extreme northeast section of Philadelphia. It's made up of two long rows of modest homes, most with owner-trimmed hedges and very old elms in their front yards. Most with swing sets or basketball hoops.

The street deadends north at St. Joseph's Church and elementary school. As Gothic cathedrals go, the church is small and unpretending. The elementary school is red-brick in color, probably large, but mostly hidden by elms.

Directly across from the school, half-hidden in still more elm trees, sits Joe Cubbah's candy store.

The name on the yellow and brown Hershey's sign says "Angie's Magazines." The candy store is called "Angie's" after Joe Cubbah's wife (who also happens to do all the work there), but in the vernacular it's "Jockey Joe's," no relation to the saint.

On that particular morning, Cubbah was minding the store for his wife.

To be more precise, he was lounging in the back booth near the pay phones.

He was equipped with steaming black coffee, cream doughnuts, *Penthouse* magazine, and the *Philadelphia Inquirer*. He was dressed in a raw silk shirt and Daks, but he smelled of bacon grease.

"Scrambled eggs, coffee, burn the rye toast—and keep it coming." A woman named Mrs. Riley was sitting at the counter giggling. Her comic material was a straight lift from a serious breakfast order the groundskeeper from St. Joe's had given Cubbah. Knowing the way Joe Cubbah operated around the store, the order had broken the neighborhood woman up.

Cubbah didn't even hear her, though. He was in the store strictly as a favor to Angela. He cleared over twenty-five thousand dollars a year, and he figured he could take or leave the six grand the little store brought in. That went double for Mrs. Riley's eighty cents a day.

"Scrambled eggs," the woman gagged on a mouthful of bialy, "coffee, burn the rye toast . . . Where's your sense of humor, Joe?"

"Shove it up your can," Joe Cubbah muttered. He looked over at the back of the woman's dirty white wedgies; he wondered how Angela could stand it all day in the store . . . But then he was watching a young priest play basketball, H-O-R-S-E, in the schoolyard; and he was back having generally good thoughts about the world.

A little after nine o'clock the day's first real customer arrived in the store. This was a rich old dentist who drilled in the neighborhood, but who lived out on the Main Line. His name was Dr. Martin McDonough.

"Hello Mister Cubbah," he called back to the pay phones. "How are you doing today?"

"Eatin," Cubbah smiled. He hitched up his trousers and started toward the front.

He leaned over the gum and cigars to talk with the dentist. "Angela tells me you're screwin around with one of those lay teachers over the school . . ."

The dentist chuckled, but he was already lost in the *Inquirer*'s sports section.

"What do you think of the Phils?" he asked.

Joe Cubbah, "Jockey Joe," didn't think of the Phils. "Seven gets you six over the Expos," he said. "Fucking Expos," he added for the fun of it. "Assholes are losing me my underwear this year."

The dentist laughed. Cubbah laughed with him. At least the old gentleman had fun losing his money.

The first bet of the day was for ten units on the Philadelphia Phillies, and "the strong right arm of Gentleman Jim Lonborg."

Coca-Cola and Wonderbread delivered their wares during the morning, and that was all that kept Cubbah from sacking out and letting Mrs. Riley run things for a while.

Wonderbread bet ten on the Philadelphia Bells over Chicago, and Coca-Cola told Cubbah that Angie was fooling around with Seven-Up. He also dropped off twelve nickel-and-dime bets from his plant.

At lunchtime Cubbah's twelve-year-old, Bennie, showed up from St. Joseph's. Bennie was supposed to help his father with the lunch crowd. This started by taking all the three-ounce hamburger patties out of the fridge, and stacking them on the counter.

"How'd you do on your big math test?" Joe Cubbah asked as they worked.

The boy bit off some Boarshead liverwurst. "Ninety-three," he said.

"Ninety-three your ass." Cubbah's face showed some pain. "What'd you get, a fucking thirty-nine, Bennie?"

The boy shrugged, smiled, talked with brown meat all

over his teeth. "Sister d'in finish correcting them. Sister Dominica had a heart attack or sum'n. So Sister Marie d'in finish correcting the math."

"So now you're all happy poor Sister Dominica had a heart attack, huh?"

"Nah . . . Well, a little bit."

Joe Cubbah laughed. Bennie was fat and funny, and sometimes he liked the little chublet better than anybody else.

Just then Cubbah looked up and saw a police detective he knew named Michael Shea. Shea was a nothing plainclothesman, but he dressed better than the mayor of Philadelphia. He was wearing a neat gray plaid suit with patent leather loafers. He was standing by the screen door, looking around like he owned the place. He nodded to Cubbah, then started to walk back toward the kitchen.

Cubbah poured two cups of coffee, then went back himself.

"Hey, sweets." Shea gave him smiling Irish eyes. "How you makin it?"

"Little of this, little of that," Cubbah said. "How's it with you?"

"Can't complain," the nattily dressed policeman said. "That your boy?" he pointed a finger and a signet ring out to the main store.

"That's Bennie," Cubbah said. He was trying to be nice. "He's failin' out of grammar school, the chooch."

Shea grinned effectively. "Listen Joey." He sat down on the edge of the stove. "I have a possible for you . . ."

"Yeah, I know," Cubbah said. "Tell me about it, Mikey."

Shea told Cubbah all that he knew—which was basically that another hired gun, a tricky, expensive guy, was being set up somewhere down South. He said someone else would be around with all the details if Cubbah took the job. They'd give him the place, and the exact time schedule he'd need to work under.

"They're offering ten plus expenses." Shea took a Danish to go with his coffee. "Somebody thought you might be the perfect guy for it."

"Yeah, that's real nice of somebody," Cubbah said. "Does this other guy have any idea somebody might be out after him?" Cubbah asked.

"My people say *no*. What the hell, I'd tell you something like that first thing out of the box."

Shea took out a thick envelope that looked like an unbelievably huge phone bill. "Half now, half later," he said. "You want it?"

Joe Cubbah shook his head slowly from side to side. "No owsies," he said.

Shea then took out a second envelope and set it down on the first. "I forgot," he grinned. "Sorry about that, sweets."

"OK," Cubbah said. He put both envelopes under his apron. "I'll think about it," he said.

He left Shea and walked out in the main part of the store again.

"Hey, wait a minute," Shea called after him. "What's this think about it shit?"

But Joe Cubbah had no more to say to the detective.

Whitehaven, July 2

Magnolias and azalias wave like high and low flags along the long, straight, whitestone drive leading up to the Powelton Country Club in the southwestern corner of Tennessee. The trees and bushes eventually open onto a grand antebellum plantation house with a great flagstone porch and thirty-foot-high Doric pillars. The ponderous building dwarfs people, motorcars, the realities of the twentieth century.

Short-haired blackmen in white coats shuffle around with silver trays holding mint julep, Jack Daniels, even Budweiser and a little Falstaff these days. Boys and girls ride and swim, play golf and tennis; and they fuck in the abandoned slaves' cabins still standing around the grounds.

For five thousand dollars annual dues, the residents of western Tennessee can enjoy the South of their daddies and mammies at the Powelton Club.

On one end of the long, flagstone porch, Johnboy Terrell sits with silver-headed Dr. Reuven Mewman, a famous veterinarian with enough cotton money to paper both ends of all the Q-tips sold in America.

People watch the two men from respectable distances. Even the black waiters watch. They all try to guess what Johnboy wants with the Silver Fox.

Terrell was puffing on a satisfying, but dangerously dark Corona. "I have recently read a very outstandin' book on vet'narians," he was saying.

"Herriot, or something on that order. *All Creatures Beautiful and Pretty*." Dr. Mewman shrugged. "I received three copies of the damn thing last Christmas. But hell John, I *see* enough horseshit without *reading* about it."

Terrell, who in addition to having an immediate use for the silver-maned animal doctor, liked him well enough, laughed heartily. Reuven Mewman, he considered, had the good timing and sense of folkiness that either made or broke orators in the South.

"Esther donated the books to a rummage sale at our church." Mewman was not one to surrender a captive audience. "They had me autograph the damn things, and charged near full price for them."

"*Then*," Mewman took bourbon and swished it around his gums, "uh woman—whose thor-uh-bred springer spaniel I saved from a overdose of Alpo last spring—presented me with a copy of one of the books I had signed, sealed, and given away to my church . . . And I *still* haven't read page one."

"Well, you ought to." Johnboy chewed and grinned. "Herriot's prob'ly the finest livin' vet'narian writin' today."

Both men laughed again and Dr. Mewman called for more drinks.

A black man who looked like Asbestos came and went, taking their reorders for double bourbons. As Mewman ordered, Johnboy watched two saddle-shoed teenagers teeing up their golf balls in front of the porch. He thought the game of golf a terrible waste of their precious youth.

"I understand," he spoke while looking out over the golf course, "that you've expressed interest in spendin a few years in Washington, District of Columbia."

"I did speak around about my availability," the veterinarian admitted. "But that was earlier this year."

"I advise against it." Terrell made a face by misshaping his lips. "Northern winters rust you . . . But I do believe," he went on, "that there's an opportunity coming up in this Senate race."

"That's because? . . ."

"That's because the one candidate, John Fair the second, is a horse's ass. Ridin high on his daddy's money plus a set of brass testicles . . . And that's because Horn . . . I understand Jimmie Horn has been seein' a white woman."

Reuven Mewman's head shook in a short arc.

"That nigger is far too smart for that, John. Too smart. Too hungry. I'm sure it'll happen one day, but not just yet . . . Where did you hear that bullshit from, John?"

Terrell watched as one of the teenagers lofted an iron shot high over two pine trees. The little white pellet dropped fifteen feet off the pin on hole number 2.

He turned in his chair to face Mewman. "I thought you were smart, also," he said. "A little smart and hungry yourself."

The veterinarian understood and he blushed a ripe, tomato red.

"You see, I'm just checking on your availability, Reuven. Because as I said, John Fair, Jr., is the original horse's ass—and Horn is vulnerable at this time."

Reuven answered the original question then. His answer came as a kind of oath. "My interest is high," he spoke. "I'd be interested and honored, John. Even to be considered, I'm honored."

Terrell stood up on the porch and shook Mewman's hand.

He left his choice for senator numb and speechless, but with two double bourbons on the way. He made his way across the front lawn, tipping his Palm Beach hat to people who still called him Mr. Governor.

PART V

"Punk"

Zebulon, November 17

One nippy, leaf-splattered Saturday in November—a week or so after a Chattanooga dentist upset a Memphis quick-food genius for Tennessee's available Senate seat—three bulging station wagons set out like Conestoga wagons in the general direction of Zebulon, Kentucky.

The people driving the individual cars were myself, my father, and Moses Reed. I was embarking on a three month L.O.A. to shore up my domestic life, and to finish the Berryman book.

The place Nan and I rented was a big, crumbling, Victorian-style farmhouse. It had its own private catfish pond, a possum hollow, and three kinds of cornfields. The owners were wintering in St. Petersburg, and the furnished, seven-bedroom house was costing us the princely sum of $105 a month to rent.

It was located exactly six miles from where I was born, and where my parents still live.

The family moved into three of the bedrooms (three of the four rooms facing down over an apple orchard and the catfish pond), and I set up two of the other rooms for my book work.

At this point I'd collected one hundred and twenty interview tapes. I had hundreds of photographs showing the story's important people as well as its key locations. There were also over a thousand pages of mimeographed notes and transcriptions from the *Citizen-Reporter*.

That winter we all took up serious ice skating and ice fishing.

I mounted a 1952 Chevy on blocks and we learned about V-8 car engines inside the barn.

Cat and Janie Bug went off to school with "a lot of creeps and hillbillies" who had become "all our friends we can't leave" by the following spring.

In general, working began to take its place in the grand scheme of eating, playing, loving, carpentering, catfishing, and card-playing at the V.F.W.

I felt I was in the right frame of mind to sit back and write something for people to read. I felt my location in Poland County gave me some pretty good perspective.

Now here's exactly what happened that first week in July.

Philadelphia, July 3

It was one o'clock in the afternoon, and as usual, Joe Cubbah was sweating like a pitcher of ice water.

Cubbah was wearing a gray sweatshirt cut off at the shoulders, and a gray fedora with what looked like a bite out of its crown.

He went into Tiny's Under the Bridge with grease all over his hands—he'd just changed the plugs and points on his Buick Electra—and he laid one hand on the shiny white rump of a twenty-year-old waitress named Josephine Cichoski.

The blond wheeled around, but when she saw it was Cubbah she only winced. She had sooty black eyelashes and thick red angel wings for a mouth.

"Your mother around?" Cubbah grinned at her. His dimples were showing and he looked kind of friendly.

"You know where." The girl pointed toward the swinging doors to the kitchen. Her big white teeth had lipstick on them.

"Hey, look who it is." Tiny Lemans blinked awake at the sound of swinging doors.

"Hey yourself," Cubbah smiled.

"Restin' my eyes here, Joey." Tiny yawned so that his mouth got big enough to fit in a grapefruit. "You're some piece of work." His eyes focused on Cubbah's sweatshirt and torn hat.

"I had to fix the Buick today," Cubbah said. "What's your excuse?"

Just then the waitress hit Cubbah in the ass with the swinging doors. Her pie-face appeared in the galley-hole, and she was sticking out her tongue.

Cubbah walked away from the door. "What's she got, a bug up her ass?"

"Fuck her," Tiny Lemans said. Fingers that were three-link sausages each tried to tie black soldier-style boots. Tiny was well over three hundred pounds.

Cubbah dipped his greasy finger in a pot of cake icing. "Goin on a trip tonight." He tasted the icing. "Oooo la, la, Tiny." He smiled at the sweetness of the icing. "Anyways ... I could use a piece. You get hold of one this quick?"

Tiny Lemans pulled out a clattering drawer of silverware. "Just got in a very nice little .38," he said. "Oooo la la." He pulled a waxed-paper package from the back of the drawer. He handed it to Cubbah intact.

"Never been fired," he said. "Airweight."

Cubbah took off the waxed paper, then held the small black revolver up to his nose. He smelled cosmo-line oil. The gun was brand new. "Just like you said it, Tiny. Very nice. *Very* nice."

"Tiny says a grasshopper can pull a fucking plow," the fat man grinned. "Hitch up that little motherfucker."

"By the way," Cubbah set down the .38. "How much is the little motherfucker costing me?"

The restaurateur yawned. "Oooo ... fuck me." His mouth opened wide again. "One hundred fifty," he said as his mouth closed.

"Too much," Cubbah said without hesitation. "Shit, I only want to *scare* somebody with this thing. You can have it back if you want."

"Look, I'm not going to fuck around with you. One thirty-five," Lemans said.

This time Cubbah took out his billfold.

Tiny waved the money away. "Put it on the Pi-rets for me. Pi-rets 7 to 8 over Yogi Berra. An' that fuck pitches Seaver you got a job *from me*. You waste Yogi Berra."

Joe Cubbah put the .38 into a brown lunch bag. He took another lick of icing and grinned.

"OK, I gotta split, Tiny. I really got to get out of state tonight," he said.

"Stick around a while," the fat man frowned. "You just got here. Have a fucking tongue sandwich. I just made some out-of-this-fucking-world tongue."

"I really have to split," Joe Cubbah said. "I really got to catch this plane tonight."

"Yeah, you gotta *scare* somebody," Tiny Lemans said.

"That's right." Cubbah held up the brown paper bag. "Right between the eyes."

Nashville, July 3

Oona Quinn was traveling south to meet Berryman.

It was a serious time for her; almost a religious time, and she didn't want it mucked up by the soldier riding beside her.

He was a baby-faced P.F.C. From Fort Campbell, Kentucky, he'd already told her. With Beetle Oil in his hair he'd told her. She'd just watched him chug a Jim Crow and Coca-Cola, and the mash whiskey and caffeine had glazed over his baby-blue mama's-boy eyes.

The two of them were seated together on an Eastern 707 flight into Nashville.

Oona had a copy of the Jimmie Horn autobiography in her lap, but she hadn't read a word since the flight started. She'd read the book halfway through the night before on Long Island. A day earlier she'd seen Ben Toy at the William Pound Institute.

Two days earlier, on the first, Berryman had called and told her to meet him in Nashville on the fourth. He'd refused to tell her why, except that he needed her there. He'd given her a place and a time, and he'd told her to dress as if she was the wife of Tennessee Ernie Ford. Then he'd hung up before she said she would or she wouldn't.

Oona was imagining Horn and Berryman meeting somewhere in the story, *Jiminy*. It would be a good chapter.

It seemed to her that Horn should win out. There had already been two attempts made on his life. A diner chef had shot at him from point-blank range and missed. Another time he'd been beaten lifeless, but had lived.

If Tom Berryman succeeded, it seemed to her, it would have to be totally unfair. Some mysterious bush-whacking. Jimmie Horn would have to end up as a martyr. She found that neither possibility bothered her. Berryman had already convinced her that the Horn shooting was inevitable. In *Jiminy*, Horn seemed to feel the same way.

She thought that she still didn't know Berryman the way she wanted to. Their relationship was too heady. All his relationships were. Maybe that was what was drawing her to him, though?

The soldier put his empty cup on her tray. "Were you all vis'tin' in New York, honey? Or are you vis'tin' in Music City? Or goin' on to Dallas maybe?"

Oona opened up her book. She pretended to read. *What I'm doing*, she thought. *I'd like to find out . . . What? . . .*

The boy swung his face down and up into her view. "I'd say. I'd *have* to say. You're vis'tin' Music City."

Oona blinked. "Excuse me?"

"Just makin' small talk," the soldier grinned. "You're goin to Nashville, I said. First time? First time, I'd bet."

"First time," she said.

"You're sure gonna like it."

The soldier grinned like the child of a brother and sister. "Country music capital of the world. Athens of the South. Home of the late President Andrew Jackson, I believe."

"Oh, did he die?" Oona said.

The soldier smiled. Bright-faced already, he lit up one of the Tijuana Smalls he'd been smoking around Times Square in New York.

"Smoke?" he asked. It was a joke. To show that, he hurriedly blew out his match. The smoke from the cigar was faintly chocolaty.

The soldier then began to tell Oona his life story. He talked whether she looked at him, or out the window. He smoked more of the little cigars, and pestered the little stewardesses for more bourbon.

"Mah, mah, mah!" they would giggle. Just "mah, mah, mah."

The jet finally began to circle over Nashville. A pencil pocket of glittering skyscrapers passed under the wing. There seemed to be a great wilderness around the main city. And Berryman was down there somewhere.

Up in the very front row of the plane, a first class stewardess was waking Joe Cubbah. She asked him to put on his safety belt. He asked her not to be ridiculous.

• • •

A green Dodge Polara was parked across the street from the American Legion Hall in Belle Meade. The car's presence meant that Jimmie Horn couldn't be far away.

At 11:15, a black detective in a white hat and blue business suit, Horace Mossman, joined two white detectives, Jerry Ruocco and J.B. Montgomery, inside the Polara.

The number of Nashville city detectives assigned to Jimmie Horn had always fluctuated between two and six, but when Horn announced his intention to run for the Senate, the number went up to eight . . . Eight detectives meant a 3-2-1 breakdown over each twenty-four hours, seven days a week. Usually, the single detective worked the eleven to seven shift.

On July 3–4, the single detective was Horace Mossman, and he was late.

"Mr. Mossman's right on his schedule," Ruocco flashed his gold-banded Timex at his partner. "Quarter hour late's just about right for Horace."

Mossman, who was in his late twenties and just recently married, smiled broadly. "It's my woman," he grinned. "She cries when I leave the house."

"Excuse me while I go throw up." Ruocco leaned over toward the young detective. Then he got out of the Polara to stretch.

Mossman shrugged, tugged on the brim of his white hat, switched on a strong penlight. He began to read the day's log on Horn.

"Anything here?" he mumbled.

J.B. Montgomery was finishing off the last of three homemade meatloaf sandwiches he'd started the night with. Montgomery's nickname among the other detectives was "Dagwood."

"He's gone to three dinners tonight," Montgomery said. "Miz Horn at six. Ne-groes worryin' about what the whites up to at eight. Whites worryin about the Ne-groes at nine. Same old shit, Horace."

Mossman grinned. He continued through the hand-written log with a red pencil ready to underline anything that struck him as abnormal.

He underlined the name *Lynch* the second time he saw it. "Who's Lynch?"

"Five foot eight or so. White hair down over his collar. Wears movie star sunglasses. Some friend of Santo Massimino."

The red pencil stopped a second time.

"And what's this 4:35?" Mossman asked. "*Hippie shakes hands with Mr. Horn. That mean something?*"

"Oh yeah ... yeah. Add uh ... add ... *unidentified long-haired man pretended to uh, jab Mr. Horn in stomach.* A little fake punch, you know the kind . . ."

Mossman had stopped writing. "Nut, J.B.?"

"Nah ... Jimmie just laughed. Seemed to know him from somewhere. He did one of those things off the boy's chin. Chip off the old block things . . . We'll check it with him tomorrow, though."

"I'll make a note," Mossman said.

"You better make the note, Horace. I should've clarified that one better."

The young black detective rewrote the note and underlined it with his red pencil. He gave it to J.B. Montgomery and the detective initialed the change.

The following evening the initialed note would appear in the *Nashville Citizen-Reporter*. So would the obituary of J.B. "Dagwood" Montgomery.

• • •

The first time I saw the UP photographs of Joe Cubbah I thought of the book *The Gang That Couldn't Shoot Straight*.

In a close-up, Cubbah looks like the author James Breslin. He looks like he should be tending bar someplace. He has an impish grin.

I bought a print of one of the UP photographs for $7.50. I'm just letting it stare up at me now. It's a weird feeling, especially the glossy gagman smile.

• • •

Cubbah got off the Eastern flight shortly after nine. A big man in a rodeo shirt met him at the gate and hand-delivered a manila envelope. Inside the envelope were sketches of Berryman that had come up from New Orleans. Cubbah examined the artwork as he rented a sports car from Avis. And because he was a cocky, fool-hardy man—the antithesis of Berryman—Cubbah signed for the car with his own name.

It's incongruous, but *under good circumstances*, Joe Cubbah would crack up most people. He has a lot of comical stories about Mafia people, and he tells them in eight or nine different accents and voices. He does the Godfather very well, but he says everybody does the Godfather. He does Carlo Gambino, and he says nobody does Gambino.

• • •

Lieutenant Mart Weesner met Cubbah under bad circumstances. At about midnight they had coffee and eggs together in a Nashville Burger Boy. Cubbah had followed the burly young trooper inside.

Weesner was in town to work the Fourth of July parade and rallies the following morning. He told Cubbah he was having trouble sleeping at the Holiday.

Joe Cubbah figured the trooper was actually out scouting up city women. Trying to score off some sympathetic waitress.

"I saw that Holiday Inn sign myself," Cubbah said. "*Welcome, B.P.O.E.*, it said. Might just as well have said *Goodbye, Joe Cubbah*. No way I was going to stay there after seeing that. Those silly bastards be practicing trumpets when the maids show up."

Weesner laughed out loud.

"What are they up to now?" Cubbah asked. "Breaking cocktail glasses in the swimming pool?"

One of the Burger Boy waitresses remembered Cubbah afterward. She remembered seeing the hefty state trooper leading him outside to show him the way to Ireland's Bar. Then she'd seen them both drive off together in the trooper's patrol car.

Ireland's is an ersatz country roadhouse; a fancy britches watering hole for rich hillbilly singers. There's a fat piano player named Dave the Rave there who's a better musician than half the millionaires in the place.

Weesner and Joe Cubbah, both up around 230 pounds themselves, watched Fat Dave like he was a limited engagement concert. Sitting together at the bar they looked like tag-team wrestlers.

Their conversation wove around two subjects: women, and the army.

"I'm in the army, 1953, stationed at Fort Bragg, North Carolina," Joe Cubbah was saying.

"What'd you make?" Weesner said.

"Didn't make nothing. I was a boxer. No rank, just boxer. I boxed a guy name of Pepper something who later got his ass kicked by Marciano. I used to box all the top MPs in bars, too."

"I boxed oranges in the navy," Weesner grinned.

"Yeah, anyways, that fat pianaman does OK for himself with the local ladies was what I was getting to. I was wondering if your uniform works pretty good for you? Southern girls used to like a uniform, I remember. I used to wear it back to Philadelphia, the girls spit on me."

Weesner laughed.

They ordered and drank another round, then Weesner slammed down a full glass of Budweiser on the bar.

"I'm getting loaded." He shook his head. "I've got to goddamn work tomorrow, do you know that?"

"Yeah." Cubbah wiped his mouth. "You got to march around with the mayor." Cubbah took up a fistful of beer nuts. "Listen," he said. "You ever eat squid? Hey, you ever heard of scungilli? . . . I'm in the mood for some squid," he laughed. "I know, you're in the mood to go back to your hotel and knock off."

"I've got to," Martin Weesner said. He stood up at the bar and called for a check.

Joe Cubbah took more nuts in his hand. He shook them around like dice.

They'd parked Weesner's police car on the side of a grocery called Scamps 400.

As they got into the blue Plymouth, Weesner, bloated, burped. "Jesus Christ!" he said. "Excuse me."

Cubbah slammed the door on his side.

"Listen," he said when both doors were closed. "I'm going to have to ask you to take off your uniform."

Weesner started to laugh, then he saw a three-to-four-inch knife in Cubbah's left hand.

"Hey Joe," he said, sober and serious in about ten seconds, "you're a real funny guy and all . . ."

Cubbah slid the sharp blade into the folds of Weesner's stomach.

"I don't want you to talk anymore. See, I'm nervous now. I could make a bad mistake. You don't talk unless I ask you a question . . . Now take your shirt off and throw it over in the back."

The state trooper had trouble with the buttons on his tight, khaki shirt. Finally, he pulled it off though. He had a surprisingly small chest with almost no hair on it.

"Now the pants," Cubbah said.

He didn't sound like he was trying to be funny, so Weesner took off his trousers. He handed them across the seat. Then he sat behind the steering wheel in his underpants, socks and shoes. He was trying to think of a plan but nothing would come.

Joe Cubbah turned on the car radio.

"Now I'm trying not to hurt you," he held the knife to Martin Weesner's throat. "Believe me I'm not," he said as ne slid the knife in, straight down, then quickly out again.

• • •

Thomas Berryman was finishing a late meal in Le Passy, one of the Middle South's most expensive and best restaurants. The dining room was extremely quiet, as it was past ten. The old wooden floors creaked softly under the footsteps of a few mincing waiters.

The third of July had been a long, busy day for Berryman; he was having trouble clearing his mind of work details. The Perfectionist in him was working overtime to luck over the Country Gentleman.

The day had begun at 8 A.M. with Berryman following Bert Poole. Poole had walked to Horn campaign headquarters once again; then he'd taken a city bus out to the big Farmer's Market: Berryman had been certain Poole was carrying the bulky .44 in his jacket. He'd walked around like Napoleon all morning long.

In the early afternoon Poole had gone home (Jimmie Horn had taken a short flight to Memphis), and Berryman had decided to switch rent-a-cars. He changed cars on the off-chance that he and the black Galaxie had been tied together. He later changed hotels for the same reason.

The new car was a blue 1974 Dart. It struck Berryman as a typical salesman's car.

The new hotel was the Holiday Inn on West End Avenue near Vanderbilt. Berryman had registered under the name Foster Benton, with the Coca-Cola Bottling Co. of Atlanta. He'd registered through July 6th.

Now Berryman savored the first sips of a cup of steaming coffee brewed with chicory.

He was thinking about his powers of concentration. Looking into the swirling coffee, he reminded himself that *because he concentrated so well*, he had a unique advantage over his opponents. He controlled the moment; they didn't. Yes, he actually did control the moment.

Then Thomas Berryman was off calculating sums of money. What was the amount he would have after Tennessee? Something above two hundred twenty thousand, he quickly figured. Tax-free cash. A tidy bankroll for Mexico.

As he sat over the coffee, he noticed his hand in the light from the table candle.

His hand was shaking.

A slight, steady, machinelike tremor made more obvious by the cup.

Berryman couldn't take his eyes off his hand.

Strong, dark fingers forced in and around the delicate Wedgwood handle. "Piano player fingers," Oona Quinn had called them. Trembling now.

A slight smile formed on Thomas Berryman's lips. "Punk," he muttered. "You punk."

PART VI

The Jimmie Horn Number

Nashville, July 4

Bert Poole woke up and found he'd slept through the Fourth of July. In fact, it was just turning to night. A cloudy, purplish night.

He stalked around breaking his Martin Luther King lamp as well as plates and cups from the kitchen. He kicked over the brown Naugahyde chair. It was so fitting he thought—after months of planning for Horn, he'd missed it. He'd never be great now—not in any way, shape or form. He went outside looking for a fight.

After a few minutes of walking, he came to a Dobb's House diner that was open.

He went inside and immediately took up hairy-eye-balling two southern hoods with gold coxcomb haircuts. The hoods were sitting over empty plates and Coke glasses. Merle Haggard was trying to tell their story over the jukebox.

When a waitress came, Poole ordered a burger with Thousand Island dressing and a milkshake.

"Oh ma-in," the girl mumbled as she scribbled the order. "Milkshake! Oh ma-in."

Poole's face was warm. His forehead was wet with perspiration.

"Ri-ight," he laid out his nervous street-person's accent. "I come in here for my dinner, ri-ight. My meal, right. And you have to hassle me, ri-ight."

The waitress put on a little smartypants smile.

"'Course most people don't ordah milkshake," she said. "Not at four ay-em in the mornin."

Poole put his hands over his face and slowly started to laugh. He peeked between trembling fingers at the Westinghouse clock over the counter. It wasn't night. He hadn't fucked it all up after all. It was ten after four ay-em.

"Bring me some black coffee, too," he said to the girl.

• • •

July 4th was announced with the usual cotton and hog reports on WKDK. Then the morning disc jockey discharged a string of fire-poppers in his studio. Then he played Johnny Cash and Tammy Wynette singing "The Star-Spangled Banner."

It was a red-hot day, and already bright at 7:30 A.M. People were wearing sunglasses like it was noon.

Wearing dark glasses himself, Thomas Berryman sat over a rib-eye and eggs at Gail's on the Turnpike diner.

But Berryman was hungrier for a little countrified bull-shit than for diner food.

A young gas-pump jockey named Uncle Smith Tarkanian finally filled the bill. Uncle Smith was no more than twenty-five; he was eating ham for breakfast: two ten-ounce ham steaks with light blue grease spread over the top.

Just relax now, Berryman was saying to himself.

"I've been playing those damn cards for about seven years now," he was saying to Tarkanian. "Knew a guy who hit six one time."

Tarkanian chewed ham and drank coffee simultaneously. "Say it like he won a fifty-thousan'-dollar lot'ry."

Both men snickered into their food. They were discussing pro football betting cards. The gas man distributed the sheets winners at his station. He was still carrying a few of the cards in his work pants.

"It's pathetic," Berryman said. "There's this guy I read. Sportswriter. He says he won seventeen thousand. Larry Merchant."

"Read the man in *Spotes Illustrated*," Tarkanian said. "He's full of shit."

"He really is."

"Has the long hair to prove it. Looks like absolute piss on old men."

"He's all of thirty-five."

"Uh-huh . . . Well, I remember this pi-ture of Lyndon Johnson and whatisname, McGovern," Uncle Smith said.

"Big Ears had a fucking ducktail on . . . What's 'at five winners on the card pay in Hot'lanta? Ten to one?"

"Fifteen. You do better parlaying it with a bookie. If they'll parlay for you."

"Fifteen ain't bad," the young man considered. "Ain't bad at all. Card works on a ninety-one percent we-win basis, my man. You should know that. You want another cup of mud there? Mrs. Bo-reen," Tarkanian shouted for their old-lady waitress, "get this man here some more of Gail's heav-en-ly coffee."

Berryman smiled. He sat at the counter looking at the backs of his hands. The shaking from the night before had passed. He lighted up a cigarillo.

"You know what," he shook the little cigar at the gas-pump jockey. "Lyndon is going to go down as one of the great presidents in the United States."

"Wouldn't doubt it," Tarkanian said. He lowered his voice. "Because pretty soon we're gonna have a nigger up there. Then a Jew. Then some goddam woman like Miss Gail cookin back there in the kitchen. Bet you."

"No bet," Berryman said. "I think you're exactly right."

"Seems I'm *always* right," Uncle Smith said, "when I don't want to be."

Berryman paid his check, then walked outside with a big smile on his face. For the moment he felt pretty level, not even any butterflies after the meal. He looked down on the turnpike and saw that it was extra busy with cars going into Nashville for the parade. He rubbed his knuckles hard against his short hair, and wondered for a minute if Oona was going to meet him.

• • •

10:30 A.M.

Horn's security got insecure on the morning of the Fourth, and young Santo Massimino later had to take adult responsibility for the mix-ups.

Nashville's wise-old-owl police chief covered his scarred flanks early in the day. Chief Carl Henry fully understood the possibilities for misadventure.

He appeared to Massimino out of the Halloween marching lines of Shriners and the Best People on Earth, and he attempted to rectify the problem of both too many chiefs and too many Indians. The scene was Dudley Field football stadium.

The old chief's mouth was open so wide a bat could have flown out of it. He was vexed, but also helpless.

"Suh. Suh, are you Mister Mass-a-mino?" he asked between nose-blowing trumpets and cymbals.

Massimino smiled and nodded without actually looking at Henry. He was planting fresh roses in the lapels of all the VIPs with seats on the speaker's dais, and he was in a dandy mood. There was good reason for this: with the mere paper promise of "celebrities" and "fireworks," he'd jammed a southern college football stadium for a black politician. (At least the stadium looked full. What most people didn't notice was that a good quarter of the seats had been cleverly masked with billboard-sized banners. But as Massimino would say, *That was, you know, show biz.*)

Henry laid kind hands on the young man's bush jacket. "The mayor axt me to talk with you," he said. "Well, actually, he didn't. But I'm going to."

The chief raised one heavy arm and pointed his wedding ring finger toward neat rows of card-table chairs sticking out of the stadium infield. "What do you think? Those are state troopers over there, aren't they?"

Massimino, who never laughed, laughed.

He held on to the liver-spotted hand of an elderly dignitary as he answered. "No disrespect meant," he said. "But I'll take the responsibility for having the governor call in state police."

"I see," Henry nodded. "You'll take the responsibility. That's good."

"The *real* problem today is going to be *over-enthusiasm*," Massimino grinned. "I wanted your men to make sure Jimmie Horn doesn't get trampled by well-wishers."

The old congressman stood looking on with his solitary rose.

Henry winked at him. He cleared his throat, took a breath. "Boy's some kind of bullshitter," he rasped.

"Well," he turned to Massimino, "I guess we'll have to live with the arrangement for today. You know," he spoke to both Massimino and the old man, "I don't want anybody shooting up his ass either."

"That's fine," Massimino said. "That's the idea."

The old man smelled his rose.

Chief Henry cleared his throat again. He backed off a step and tapped his walkie-talkie. "You keep in touch, Santo."

Henry then gazed off into the buzzing grandstands like a Roman general at the Colosseum. Today, he was a loser for some ungodly reason or another. "Those state boys give out speeding tickets right well," he chatted idly. "But I wouldn't depend on'm for too much more."

The old man VIP coughed out a laugh at that remark. "I wouldn't depend on'm," he tugged Massimino's sleeve, "findin' they'ah zippers to pee."

•   •   •

Joe Cubbah talked to himself as he paced the ranks of folding metal chairs.

Cubbah was melting. He had sweat stains halfway down to his Sam Browne, and his kinky black curls were dripping on the shoulder patches of Martin Weesner's uniform. They didn't have fucking inhuman weather like this in Philadelphia, he mumbled. Some asshole had told him it was a hundred and fifteen degrees down on the field. The temperature dropped ten to fifteen degrees just walking in the shade of the speaker's platform.

He nudged a redheaded boy sipping Ripple wine in the open, and the youngster obediently tucked away his bottle. He even said he was sorry.

"Man, don't ever say you're sorry," Cubbah advised. "Just be more careful. Be more careful, see."

Keeping an eye out for Thomas Berryman, he continued to circle in closer to the speaker's dais. He enjoyed the way the country crowds parted for his uniform. He thought he understood why mountain boys leave home to become sheriffs.

Inside the locker room marked VISITORS, Jimmie Horn was sitting by himself at the far end of a long golden bench. The bench ran along in front of golden lockers, all of them filled with golden shirts and helmets.

As is the standard procedure in the Southeastern Football Conference, the locker room floor was covered with wall-to-wall carpeting.

Twenty or more men and women were standing around the room but none of them were talking. It was like a hollow cell at the center of all the football crowd noise.

At 10:35 Jimmie Horn's press secretary went over to the mayor. He performed a ritual that often went on with Horn before big speeches.

He knelt so that his face was down even with Horn's. "It's twenty-five minutes to eleven now," he whispered.

Jimmie Horn only nodded.

At 10:45 the press secretary repeated the procedure, giving Horn the new time.

Jimmie Horn nodded, spoke the man's name, and stood up.

Now the twenty-odd people in the room began to talk. Laughter started up. "All right. All right. All right now." Santo Massimino began to pace and clap his hands.

After a few minutes, Massimino walked up to Jimmie Horn and asked him what he was thinking about.

Horn smiled at him. "You really need to know?" he said.

"Yeah," Massimino said. "I need to know."

"Well . . . I was in a rowboat, fishing out on Lake Walden," Horn said. "It was a pleasantly cool day; I kept dipping my arms in the lakewater . . . I caught some catfish, and some nice bass, Santo. Sometimes, though, the fishing isn't so good out there."

When Jimmie Horn appeared in the dark eye of a concrete tunnel entrance to the field, Joe Cubbah ran ahead and joined the six or seven city policemen who crossed over to meet the mayor.

Jimmie Horn was tall, stately, but Cubbah thought he looked a little nervous.

Cowboys, two roadhouse bouncers outfitted in chambray shirts, came riding by firing blanks. Cubbah was so startled he wheeled and nearly shot one of them off his horse.

●　●　●

Each little detail seemed both extremely important, and extremely unimportant, to Thomas Berryman.

He took out a thick, black, garrison belt. The belt was about three inches in width. He looped it around his rib cage, then pulled it as tight as he could stand it. The pressure made him burp on his breakfast.

A risk should be taken now, he was thinking. Some of his calmness at breakfast was gone; some of the shaking from the night before had returned.

He picked up the hotel room's desk chair. Stood it up on the bed. Flush against Versailles garden in the wallpaper.

He removed velveteen couch cushions and carefully stacked them on end across the desk chair.

Finally, he fluffed all three bed pillows and punched them in tight, punched them in front of the couch cushions. The back of the chair was up level with his face now. At chin level.

Berryman measured the distance across the room to the door.

He unlatched it. Looked up and down the halls where black chambermaids were up to their morning cleaning business. There was some sisterly chattering and some vacuuming, but it was fairly quiet and orderly in the hotel corridor. It smelled slightly of the dust being raised. Perfumed dust.

Standing in the open doorway, Berryman raised the .44 magnum revolver with its silencer. He braced the handle tightly against the garrison belt.

Occasionally checking the cleaning women with glances, he rehearsed the fast motion of raising and lowering the gun to belt level.

He fired off two shots with the gun pressed against his ribs. The distance from the doorway to the chair was about sixteen feet.

The gunshots destroyed the bed pillows, blowing dust and feathers all over the room.

The nearest maid was two doorways away. She was draping white towels over her arm. Scooping a handful of soap bars. Humming. The two muffled *pfftts* had gone unnoticed in the hall.

Berryman shut the door. He sat down and took off the belt. The recoils had left a slight, livery bruise on his ribs. His stomach was quivering.

The hunting pistol was unwieldy and overly nasty, but it would work for the job. He hoped that his central nervous system would function half as well.

• • •

Husky, bowlegged farmers sauntered along Nashville's sidewalks with their thumbs in their belt loops.

Their wives held pinwheels or Nashville pennants or rabbit balloons; they used the toys to point out the monuments of President Andrew Jackson and Henry Clay.

Their children seemed more impressed with what the parade horses had left in the streets.

That fact of life amused the farmers almost as much as city life did.

Thomas Berryman sat at a stoplight on West End Avenue. The light changed and he straddled the tracks of a peppy Volkswagen. Five hippie girls in the bug.

He took the Dart over two quiet single-block streets—one west, one south—and when he turned onto a wider avenue, he tested the car up to fifty-five. Another little precaution.

Black people began to appear down another quiet street. A crazy-looking old woman was boiling clothes in a washpot.

Three teenagers bopped along in black shirts and porkpie hats, looking like fugitives from the law.

A large blackman lounged in a white convertible with the radio blaring "R-E-S-P-E-C-T."

Berryman finally parked on a hill overlooking Bert Poole's building. Now for the proof of the pudding.

As he came down the hill, Thomas Berryman smelled fish frying. Once again he noticed the black Marlboro cowboy.

He buttoned his green shirt and tightened the green and red Christmas tie. He waited until he got to the pink house itself before he slipped into the green Bond's suitjacket.

Dressed the way he was, Thomas Berryman looked like a character out of James T. Cain.

Bert Poole answered the door wearing only blue-jeans and green wool socks.

He didn't have a chest or stomach, just a straight plumb-line drop from his chin to his toes. His belly button was protruding like a small wart.

Loud music was coming from inside the apartment.

"I'm Marion Walker," Berryman said. "Sorry to have to bother you on a holiday. I'm with the Cain-Sloan Department Stores."

He handed Poole one of the business cards he'd been collecting around Nashville. It said *Marion A. Walker*, Cain-Sloan Co.

Bert Poole looked troubled and confused at first, then he started to smile.

"Damn," he spoke in a soft, polite hippie's voice, "they don't even let you guys rest on a holiday, do they?"

Berryman shook his head. "No sir, they don't. They been tryin to reach you all over the place I guess. People at home more on the holidays. That's how the F.B.I. catches deserters, I heard."

Poole started to look past Berryman into the street. Three little black kids passed the house on Easy Rider bikes. "Well, you got me," Poole said. "I guess you want your record player and your chair?"

"Don't know anything about a record player," Berryman said—he'd only seen a bill for a chair when he'd visited the apartment. "I'm afraid you do owe us on a Naugahyde recliner though. Brown Naugahyde. You never did make a payment on that one."

Bert Poole started to laugh. He crouched forward holding his bare arms, rubbing them up and down. "You're taking that chair right now?" he managed.

Berryman scratched at the front of his short haircut. He shook his head.

"I don't personally pick up any furniture," he said. "Our men would like to pick it up today though."

Bert Poole suddenly turned serious again. "Today's out," he said.

Berryman squinted distrustfully. "What's the matter with today? You're here, aren't you?"

"I work for Mayor Horn," Poole quickly said. "I can give you the chair right now. Either that, or you have to wait . . . I'm working with Mayor Horn from one-thirty until I don't know what time today. That's how come I've been too busy to pay. I really have the money." Poole started to come apart before Berryman's eyes.

Berryman started scratching his head again. The one thing he didn't want to do was spook the young hippie. He smiled.

"Well, just fuck'm," he said to Poole. "They can wait 'til tomorrow for their chair. Fuck'm . . ." Berryman shook his head as though he was embarrassed. "I'm just sorry to have to bother you like this . . . on a holiday."

"Well, I'm sorry you had . . . I'm sorry I made you come out here," Bert Poole's soft hippie voice returned. He was smiling now too. "It's your holiday, too, isn't it? Don't forget about that."

The two men shook hands on the porch and Berryman noticed the time. It was 11:45. Poole was going to be out of the house by one-thirty. It was getting very, very close, Berryman thought. It was all going to fall into place just about right.

• • •

Horn's staff was trying to be careful. Conscientious and smart.

Right after his speech, they hustled the popular mayor out of Dudley Stadium like an unpopular Saturday afternoon football referee. A gray limousine was waiting, and the air conditioner had it ice cold. Big sweaty men pressed inside the car like sides of beef. Eight of them.

The mayor's speech had gone extremely well; Santo Massimino had delivered on nearly all of his arrogance; but you wouldn't have guessed it from the conversation.

Horn had been pushed in back between his advance-man Potty Lynch, an alderman, and a black secret service man named Ozzie. The mayor was squirming.

"What is . . . uh . . . going on here?" he kept projecting his soft voice into the front. He was clearly agitated by the unexpected state troopers at Dudley Field. Also by the state Cadillac. And by Ozzie. "Where's the parade convertible?" he asked, "and what is going on?"

The chauffeur carefully guided the big car through the quiet stadium back lots. The limousine passed through rows of orange school buses. Through spotless alleyways. Under brick arches and hanging vines. The car glittered everywhere.

"No more convertibles." Jap Quarry smiled at his friend's question. "Parade's over, baby."

"They don't make convertibles in Detroit anymore," the alderman said.

Santo Massimino, New Yorker masquerading as Californian, was studying the windshield like it was an important map.

At that point, the chauffeur took two wheels of the Cadillac *bang-thud* over a hump of sidewalk.

Everyone thought *gunshot*. All eight men were disconnected for a minute.

When the car wheels were properly on the road again, Horn lit up a cigarette. In between slow puffs he cracked a few jokes about his naiveness. About everyone else's bad nerves.

Potty Lynch eventually turned sideways and started to give him his good, blue-eyed donkey advice. Lynch had ridden in cars with the Kennedys, he said.

"Jimmie, listen to me." He was Pat O'Brien incarnate. "See, the ball's in our court. See, we're experienced in this incredibly miserable shit. We have to watch out for you. Because *you won't* be able to watch out for yourself."

This Boston posturing only served to set Horn off again. Maybe it was because Lynch's attitude was so know-it-all.

"What's this *we?*" Jimmie Horn asked in the habitually sweet-sounding voice. "Do you have a frog in your pocket?" he toyed with the veteran. "What's this *we* stuff, Jap? *You* won't mind telling me?"

Jap Quarry only laughed. "This man's trying to be your friend, don't you see," he said without turning to the back. "Besides, the whole affair's going to be too big to start bringing your own personal feelings in. Join the Horn team, man."

Horn looked around and deadpanned the secret service

man. "I'm . . . uh . . . James Lee Horn," he said, "and I'm running for United States Senator. I'm awful glad to meet you."

The secret serviceman had a surprisingly human laugh. "I'm not a Tennessee resident," he cracked.

Santo Massimino finally turned around. He lowered tinted sunglasses onto a large, pocked nose. "Very, very nice speech back there," he grinned. "You're very good."

Horn smiled softly. He patted his haircut.

As the limousine waited quietly under a red light at West End Avenue, a motorcycle escort swept up on both sides. The cycles stopped extremely close, idling within an arm's length of the car.

Silent *three ring* and *lead on, Lochinvar* signs were exchanged back and forth through the windows. Sirens wailed, then wailed again at a higher pitch. The small motorcade ran all the other traffic lights to midtown and Roger Miller.

As they reached Tenth Street a green and white Country Squire shot up alongside of them. Jimmie Horn looked out, frowned, then smiled into the lens of a hand-held Arriflex movie camera.

• • •

Noon. The air-raid siren had begun to blend into each Nashville afternoon. Oona Quinn walked down a quiet shady street outside of Dudley Field. Her mind was a blank. Seeing Horn in the flesh, watching him deliver his speech inside the stadium had panicked her. She wanted to talk to Berryman, but she didn't know where to find him until 3:15.

Less than a mile away, Thomas Berryman was standing in an open field with his arms outstretched. Listening to the grass grow.

He was thinking that it was the experience of peyote that had taught him to relax, and conversely had probably started Ben Toy on his road to going crazy. He was remembering different things about Toy as he watched a coven of Catholic nuns and some school-age lovers counting the front steps of Centennial Park's ludicrous Parthenon.

Berryman's eyes parted company with the dull sheep, and traveled with the dark ladies.

They walked the great stone walls to an edge, then stood still, as though they'd come to the very end of a gangplank. They seemed to be praying for the world's leapers. Praying for them, or trying to understand them.

Berryman had taken a light downer, and he was calm enough to feel a falling body float, even swim. Talking to himself he said: *I'll walk around here until two. I'll get a sandwich. Black coffee. Then I'll split.* Basically, he was on autopilot now.

He was carrying a transistor radio and he begrudgingly tuned in a bulletin about the parade and rally at the football stadium. It was reported that Horn and his family had already been taken downtown. It was speculated that extra security precautions were being taken around Horn.

Berryman switched on music and walked around kicking kickweed, blowing blo-balls, talking to the different people who pleased his sense of composition in the park. This relaxing was a ritual with him. It was necessary.

When he left the park he was as cool as he could have hoped to be.

Oona Quinn, meanwhile, was hiring a city cab to take her out to the junction of Kingsbridge Highway and Fullerton Avenue. That was where the Farmer's Market was; it was where Jimmie Horn was going to make his next public appearance; and it was where Berryman had asked her to meet him.

From 2:10 on she sat in the Lums restaurant at the Market Plaza. She was wearing a J.C. Penney pantsuit that blended very nicely into the crowd. Then, at 2:30, Oona Quinn decided to telephone her father.

• • •

Random Observation (Jap Quarry's):
   "I think one of the evil things you'll find on television," Quarry said to me one slow afternoon after the shooting, "is this practice of showing news films of the so-called violent events. They're like circuses on television. Like some novel form of entertainment.

   "These films don't recreate the way it feels. They create false feelings.

   "The news clips of Jimmie's shooting, for example. They didn't recreate any truth for me. There was nothing, *let's-all-sit-back-and-be-objective* about the actual scene. In reality it was a fucking disgrace.

"On the other hand, I can remember the way TV portrayed the death of Lyndon Johnson.

"That was sad. That had dignity. It gave you a feeling for what had occurred. For the way his people may have felt.

"Maybe it's because I have a touchstone in my experience for deaths in the family, but not for wholesale shootouts.

"Maybe these TV shootouts will begin to pass for touchstones. That's what I'm afraid of sometimes."

• • •

The rally at the Fair Farmer's Market was calculated to cookie-cutter black voters out of the large, doughy black bread of Tennessee. It was a carbon copy of rallies Santo Massimino had held in municipal parking lots in Newark, and in trucking yards in Roxbury, Mass.

By two-thirty, adventuresome families had lined up across the Better Crust bakery and the jewelry and dime store rooftops. Little flying dresses were playing tag on one roof. What good was it to come, they seemed to have all decided, and not see Jimmie Horn in Technicolor.

Rows (there were actually small lines) of school-age boys boosted one another up on greasy tractor trailers, and even onto the buckling Dr Pepper and Wrigley's advertising billboards.

It was hectic and exciting, but also pretty in a democratic way.

The market lies five hundred feet beneath Snake Hill, and from the hill's crest it's said by local people to look like a *county fair on fire*.

Coming down off the hill, pushing his way through waist-high grass, stumbling on hidden rocks—kicking them with his boot heel—Bert Poole had the strange feeling that he was walking in a foreign country. Someplace like Jamaica or Brazil.

Poole's attention kept drifting away from the podium.

He looked down on families of ten and twelve people—sharecropper antiques—shuffling across a nearby farmer's field. Some of the children trampled tomatoes. Danced on them. Threw them back and forth like sponge balls.

Poole looked back to the dais. It was up on a level with the Commercial Southern bank roof, and up over the people standing on the bank roof was the white eye of the hottest sun of the summer.

A small man with a plump, pink head stood at the podium microphone with his thumbs in his belt like a baseball manager.

"Mrs. Betty Lou Rice is eighty-two years young," he

announced over the happy background of carnival noise. "This week. This week of July fourth. She has walked. She has walked over one hundred miles. To come and see her young prince. That is Jimmie Horn."

Applause. Applause. Right-ons.

"As a younger woman, Mrs. Rice just told me, she did the same thing ... To meet Mister Huey Long of Louisiana."

Boos. Louder applause.

White-shirted managers of the Plaza stores were lined up to give the old black woman gifts like a pair of black-tie grandmother shoes. She didn't look as if she knew exactly where she was, but wherever it was, it was swell, and worth a big grin. "Jim-mah Hone" was the only thing she ever said.

The four Cadillacs seemed to float into the sea of hands. The sun made stars and circles off the chrome, and the steel guard tires made a sound like a sticky tape being pulled up off linoleum.

Young Massimino and Potty Lynch trooped man-of-the-people style in front of Horn's car. They waved and smiled as though everyone in town knew them.

Joe Cubbah was last in one line of three husky troopers flanking the limousines. He searched the crowd for Berryman, holding the limousine door handle so he wouldn't lose track of the car.

Ten-year-old Keesha, and teenager Mark Horn, were laughing and dangling out the windows of the car ahead of their parents. The lead car carried Horn's own mother and father.

Smiling black faces and arms were disappearing inside the rear windows, ready to shake hands with any of them, knowing that if they succeeded, they would later claim it had been Jimmie.

Naturally enough, Jimmie Horn was happiest and at his best among predominantly black crowds. He felt he could loosen up and show more of himself—be a person instead of a phenomenon.

Black people, especially country folks, liked to touch Horn to make sure he was real.

They wanted him to touch them too, especially their children, and tell them they were going to be doctors or lawyers or teachers. Sometimes when Horn bent and spoke to a child specially dressed to meet him, the child's mother or grandmother would start to cry.

But it was too noisy for Horn to be heard that afternoon in the Farmer's Market. Smiling black faces mouthed complicated-looking sentences at him, but he just shook their hands and held their hands, and ran his big hands through the fluffy hair of their children.

When he let go of one smiling, hollering boy he found the boy had left him a photograph.

It was of a black family of eighteen or twenty members all dressed in suits and organdy dresses and men's and women's felt hats. They were all posed with a cantankerous-looking Marblehead Horn, standing in front of the old man's run-down grocery.

The back was carefully signed by each family member and then by Jimmie Horn's own father.

Bert Poole accepted a peppermint-striped straw hat from one of the *Schoolgirls for Jimmie*, and he put it on as he continued to walk sideways through the crowd.

He stopped in front of two young white boys. Each was wearing a battered George Wallace hat. From the looks of their faces, neither had a measurable I.Q.

"Trade you this new hat," Poole smiled. "For one of those old ones. Just one. You keep the other."

The boys looked at one another and started laughing.

"Nuh," the taller one finally answered. "We ain't jig lovers."

Bert Poole smiled again. "Ri-ight. 'Course not," he said. "I'll give you some money for the hat."

Once again the boys looked at one another. As if there was only one brain for the two of them. "How much is *some?*"

Poole took off the Horn hat and put a dime store wallet inside it. "Take what you think's fair," he told the taller boy. "Don't take any more than that."

Each boy took two dollars and they ran like hell.

Nearly all the shops along the Plaza were closed and dark, and women were using the blackened windows as mirrors.

Even the airfield hangar of a supermarket—OPEN 24 HOURS, 365 DAYS OF EVERY YEAR—was cleared of all but a few deadfaced shoppers.

A lighter flared in one of the grayish windows. Not the usual gold Cartier, a Gillette Cricket.

Thomas Berryman drew on a cigarillo as he looked on through red FARMER DRUGS lettering.

Berryman was playing a mind-game with himself: he was thinking about all of the jobs he'd completed successfully. He was figuring out exactly how they compared with this one; degree of difficulty they called it in those high-diving contests. The thing he didn't trust about this plan was that it was so spectacularly different from all the others. Either it was brilliant, or it was foolish; and even though he was ninety-nine percent sure it was the former, he could have done without the latter 1%.

Then tne idea of dying, actually dying, powered through his mind. The idea used so much energy that his mind shut off and went blank for a moment.

He focused on the neon FARMER DRUGS lettering. He wondered if Oona had shown up. That would make it easier. A man and his wife wouldn't be stopped after the shooting. All the better if she was crying.

The red neon and the weak light behind the prescriptions window were the only ones left on in the store. "Closin' up," the druggist called from the rear of the store. "Closin' for the speeches. Open up at four."

Berryman cradled the magnum revolver in a blue windbreaker over his arm. The rest of his outfit was the pea-green shirt and tie, and the green suit pants. He was silent and pensive. A little nervous now.

He finally flipped the cigar behind the greeting cards

rack. Stepped on it. Tightened the garrison belt inside his shirt.

The druggist coughed and Berryman ignored him. Then he stepped out of the cool store and started pushing through the good-natured crowd like somebody important.

Joe Cubbah had gotten a tremendous headache. Moreover, he had the runs.

The sun was white hot, but he had his sunglasses off. He had to make facial distinctions, and he couldn't do that, or judge depth, through the dark glasses.

The sun was directly in his eyes and pain grew from the bridge of his nose like a small, spreading tree.

He thought he'd found Berryman. But Berryman was walking with his back to the sun. He was extremely hard to look at.

He was pushing his way up through the crowd—being very unsubtle—and Cubbah didn't get it. He could see the blue windbreaker and thought it concealed a gun. He'd snapped the button on his own holster, Weesner's; he had his hand on the unfamiliar service revolver. He thought he might shit in his pants.

Berryman was saying something. Saying something, then smiling. People were clearing out of the way for him. He was only about ten rows away, and if it hadn't been so noisy, Cubbah would have been able to hear whatever he was saying to get through.

He slipped the service revolver nearly all the way out.

He was sweating like he was being cooked, trying to keep track of both Horn and Berryman, trying to control his bowels, squinting very badly, when Berryman stepped all the way into the sun.

• • •

The pudgy master of ceremonies laughed and clapped his hands like a seal. "Whutat under yay?" he called down from the podium.

Horn couldn't hear or understand. He smiled. Looked elsewhere.

Black people were drinking lemonade. Grinning as though someone was taking wedding pictures. They slouched on one foot. Squinted under the sun. Wiped their foreheads with their sleeves and brown paper bags.

The noise made it easy for Horn to retire inside himself. Relax for a minute before his speech. *It was a long field of striped cotton. Four o'clock of a day that had begun in the dark. There was a party for some undiscoverable reason. Everybody was forgetting everything. His grandmother, however, was out walking in the bright sun. She avoided shadows like a fly.*

A college boy pumped his hand with embarrassing enthusiasm. These younger men in the crowd, Horn was sure, had dreams of going up on fancy platforms like the one before him. He'd had those dreams at times. Dreams of having his important (at least sensible) words amplified a half a mile. Of getting the attention, eyes, of five thousand faces. Of wearing suits that made you look as good as you knew you could.

The m.c. tapped his thumb against the microphone. It coughed. " . . . eesha? . . . " he called off the mike.

Keesha? His little girl?

Horn smiled again. Waved to Charles Evers while his eyes were up on the platform. Evers smiled. He couldn't hear either. Slouched over a card-table chair, he looked like he was waiting for a train.

Jap Quarry shouted down from the stage. Encouragement. Baseball catcher *rah, rah*.

Horn's fingers were following a prickly restraining rope leading to the stairs of the platform. He was smiling at the faintly familiar receiving line. His wife pinched his elbow. Someone did.

Applause rose as he got closer to the stairs.

Then it fell. Sank. Faces and clothes flashed by him like laundry in a washer. Lights winked, one of them the sun.

Two strings of gun*pops* seemed to happen in another dimension of sound. There were five more *pops*, then four more. Then two more. There were flashbulbs that sounded like more shots, but looked more frightening than the actual shooting.

The master of ceremonies stood still, his mouth was gaping. He thought he was shot himself. His picture was taken.

Many people thought they'd been shot. Several had been.

Jap Quarry finally took charge of the microphone. He looked down at Horn, never once out at the crowd. The pauses between his sentences were lengthy. "A doctor is up here already." "The sniper is a white man." "Please clear back. Please . . . *You* get back there, mister."

Oona Quinn was up close. She'd seen Berryman.

"If you don't give Jimmie air," Quarry said, "he'll die right here on us."

The great craning of necks was followed by the spectacle of people running around with their arms spread out like wasps. Running, flapping wings.

Little girls hugged their mothers and were hugged right back. Old people held one another up from falling. Big men sat on the top of tractor trailers and cried on their shoetops.

One old social worker went onto her black stockings on the platform. She swayed, swayed—reciting "Thou art my good and faithful servant in whom I am well pleased."

Oona Quinn watched a man's bare, hairy leg for several minutes. She knew he was a policeman. Shot in the stomach by another policeman.

She saw Poole where he'd been shot down. A thin, curly-headed boy with no more nose or right eye. Frozen deranged. A broken straw hat was pulled down over his eyes like a gambler's visor.

All along she'd watched Mrs. Horn.

They pulled her back from him. She had blood on her nose and cheek.

As she rose, Jimmie Horn slowly came into sight.

The bones in his forehead had been splintered, piercing out through the skin like miniature broken ribs. There was sweat all over his face, and the sweat beads looked like blisters. He was saying something in a soft voice that seemed unrecognizable to his wife.

Two pale hospital attendants ran with a feathery litter, then ran with him dead.

As he'd known he would from the beginning, Thomas Berryman had succeeded.

PART VII

The Thomas Berryman Number

Louisville, December 8

I'm sitting in the largest farmhouse bedroom, drinking Johnny Walker Scotch. Mostly I'm considering the final interview I had. But I'm also thinking that you never really know who lied to you along the way. Who led you down a wrong road. You just get someplace. This is it.

Institutional gray buildings had blended into foothills that were just about blue. They were smoke-colored. Negro men ran in a yard that was visible from the neighboring streets. They seemed to be practicing professional football drills. This impression struck me as illogical at first. Then slightly logical as I thought about it. I had come to the federal penitentiary at Louisville.

I parked the Audi outside the front gates. Across from an apple-red gas station. It was cool. A day for carcoats. It was a Saturday in early December.

Walking toward the somber gray buildings, I thought about this book as a whole.

It seemed odd to me that there is no discernible pattern to personality, but that readers come to expect cause and effect. I myself expected cause and effect as a reader.

Well, I was short on causes—so maybe I had achieved some sort of realism. Or maybe I just hadn't dug deep enough. I wasn't really sure.

I thought about my daughter, Cat, then. At that time, whenever I thought about her and she wasn't around, I came to a remark she'd made a few weeks earlier. She'd said, "Ochs, when I go to the supermarket now, people shooting guns always comes into my mind." On Saturdays (Saturday is Nan's shopping day), Cat had been sleeping late or starting to vacuum or dust if her mother even mentioned going to shop.

A tall, balding guard at the front gate asked me who I was there to see. He didn't ask me to "state my business," or anything like that. He was sipping coffee, very cordial and friendly.

"My name is Jones," I said. "I'm here to see Joseph Cubbah. My newspaper has already contacted your warden."

• • •

(Interview between Ochs Jones and Joseph Cubbah. Taped at the federal penitentiary at Louisville.)

Jones. Do you mind if I ask questions?

Cubbah No. No, that's a good way. Yeah . . .

J: I uh . . . What were your feelings about Bert Poole? For
starters.

C:Who's Bert Poole?

J: I'm sorry . . . The young hippie boy in Nashville. The
boy you . . .

C: None. Nothing.

J: If you could think of anything? . . .

C: . . . He was an asshole. (Laughs) Really.

(I felt that Cubbah thought I was trying to draw some kind
of half-assed parallel here. I abandoned the topic.)

J: . . . All right . . . What about Berryman? Tell me what
happened?

C:In actual fact, he got fucked over. I don't know, you
know . . .

J: Not exactly . . . Any specifics you . . .

C:He was double-crossed. See, he was in the crowd
there . . . Hey, why don't you make sure your tape's
working . . .

J: It is. I can see the thing turning . . . I'll play it . . .
(Click) . . .

C: That's me, huh?

J: I'm always surprised at the way my voice sounds . . .
It's on . . .

C:Yeah, well, Berryman was in the parking lot. I was
watching him when the other kid . . .

J: You're talking about Bert Poole?

C:Bert Poole, he opened up right in front of me. Maybe I was a row of people away from him. When it happened, you know, I figured he was working with Berryman. I don't know *what I thought*. He never hit Jimmie Horn, though. Didn't even know how to hold a gun.

J: What happened to Horn? Do you know? . . .

C:Berryman hit him. Shot right through this wind-breaker. He had a windbreaker over his arm. Two shots, I figure. Silencer. *Pfft. Pfft.* .44. Which I don't understand to this day. Neat trick.

J: You shot Poole though? . . .

C: That was just an accident. Reflexes. See, I already had my hand on the gun. But when I turned around for Berryman, he's already gone. Back in the crowd. I couldn't believe it. Like ten seconds of the greatest fucking confusion in my life. Everybody's screaming. There's movie cameras all over Horn. He's shivering. Keeps kicking the back of his heel into the asphalt. Like these little kicks. This is fifteen, twenty seconds. I swear to Christ.

J: I've seen films, Joe . . .

C:Yeah.

J: What did you do then? I'll try not to interrupt.

C:Fuck it, that's OK. After that? Well, I got my bearings first of all. Then, I started to make my way back through the mob. Saw Berryman going into the big market there with this girl. Long-hair girl. Tall one. I walked in behind them, both of them, and he's filling up a cart.

Actually filling up a fucking grocery cart with fucking steaks and Rice Krispies. This girl's cool. She looks cool, I mean. But I can tell she's nervous. You can tell. She does these little things like brush her hair back too much. Berryman can tell, too. At least something's bothering him. He keeps telling her to shut up. He's so mad he looks like he's blushing or something. Anyway, they get together all these groceries—two or three bags at least—and then they go outside like it's home to baby.

J: They left?

C: Hell no. Because outside is this huge traffic jam. They have to sit tight in the car. I sit tight myself. Take a dump I've been holding in for hours. Try to figure out what I should do . . . Please . . . (Sound of lighter snap) . . . (Splice in tape) . . . Around four-thirty. Thereabouts. It gets dark and starts to rain like a bitch. The air gets cleaned. I get cooled off. It's terrific. I hop into the drugstore. Buy a big black umbrella. Stand around outside like Potsy the Cop.

J: Berryman's still stuck?

C: Of course. He's finally out in an aisle though. Right up alongside this cyclone fence. Like leaving the drive-in. I go up to the car and bang on the window.

J: Does he know you?

C: No. He looks out to see who it is. Opens the window about an inch for me. "Put your window down," I yell over the rain. It's pounding like hell on the umbrella. Teeming. You can't see shit it's so gray. "Hey, you know it's pouring rain?" he yells. Something like that. His girlfriend's as cool as ice, though. She's beginning to worry me. "You know your brake lights aren't working," I say. He smiles very polite at this point. He's really smooth as silk, I can tell. So when he opens the door about three feet I immediately hit him in the heart. "Hey man," he says. He's dead before I pull the knife. The girl is yelling, but mostly drowned out by rain on the roof and maybe a little thunder. I slapped her right in the face. "You don't want to wind up in the joint," I tell her—*jail*, I think I said. "You get him the fuck out of here." The girl just about stops crying. She gets something like the hiccoughs.

J: You're talking about . . . like, hi-*cup?* . . .

C: Yeah. Right.

J: What happened then?

C: That's the most beautiful part of it. Nothing happened. I waited for the lot to clear out a little. Stood around thinking about his girlfriend. How she's going to handle it. How I'm going to handle the ten grand. That's what you always think about. Every time. They should give me a medal, no? . . .

January of the Following Year

Early in January, sitting upright in a canvas beach chair at the Royal Biscayne Hotel in Key Biscayne, a copy of *National Geographic* in his lap, Johnboy Terrell felt a brief, sharp pain at the center of his chest. His head dropped sharply and his wife said something. He thought he was throwing up his breakfast until he saw blood all over his lap. He died right there in the beach chair, his jury trial not having reached the courts yet.

And then late on another day in January, a cold, dark one, Thomas Berryman's body was uncovered by three schoolboys and a girl. They were sleighing in a cow pasture behind a Quality Court motel in Asheville, North Carolina. The body had been covered over by a mound of hay.

There were no clothes on the body, but it had been wrapped in two woman's dresses. The stomach and feet were exposed, and they were crusted with black blood.

The boys ran to the nearest house. They told a housewife that a skinny old man was dead in Skinner's Field. They skipped the part about the woman's dresses.

Two deliverymen in the neighborhood went with them to look at the body. They too thought it was an old man. The housewife they told came with a pocket camera and took a picture.

A deputy sheriff found men's clothes and various forged identifications nearby.

Ochs Jones
Zebulon, Kentucky

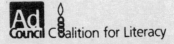